I0543358

QUICKBANE

PART ONE · NOVELLA

Chelsea Starling

© 2014 Chelsea Starling

This is a work of fiction. the characters, names, places, incidents and dialogue are products of the author's imagination and are not to be construed as real.

No part of this book may be reproduced in any form whatsoever without prior written permission of the publisher except in the case of brief passages embodied in critical reviews and articles.

ISBN: 978-0-9904975-0-9

Distributed in the U.S.A.

Chelsea Starling
Charlottesville, VA 22901

www.chelseastarling.com

Cover art by Yu Cheng Hong
Formatted by Courtney Nuckels
Edited by Christina Mercer
Proofread by Typo Killer

For every person who struggles with depression, anxiety or PTSD.
Never give up. I believe in you.

PROLOGUE

Jesobel

"Push, Jasmine! The baby is almost here!"

The laboring woman waited for a deep contraction to wrap around her belly and tighten like a boa constrictor. When the tightness became unbearable, she tensed every muscle in her body. She bore down and pushed.

A guttural wail, rising in crescendo along with her pain, rang out across the hills. Dogs barked and people working outside startled and dropped their tools. For a moment, the whole marketplace fell silent.

"I can't do this!" she screamed. Her body shook with fatigue; sweat poured down her face. The heat of the tent suffocated her, and she gasped for a breath of cool air in vain. The hours passed slowly, and it seemed she had been laboring two whole days inside the tent.

"You can, Jasmine," urged Agnes, squeezing the young woman's hand with her own time-worn fingers. "You're almost there!"

"You said that this morning! I can't," she cried. "I can't do it."

Jasmine twisted the birthing rope around her forearms until she could hang in a deep squat for a moment. Myriam sat behind her on her knees and massaged Jasmine's aching sacrum.

"Every woman feels this way, it's okay. One more push, and this baby will be in your arms. Don't give up now, Jasmine!"

Jasmine gathered the remainder of her strength. There was very little left after fifty-two hours of labor. Her body felt as if it would rip in two. She felt the energy leaving her legs; her thighs quivered with exhaustion.

Shanshono shosho, shoshono fheelo, shosho shosho shosho. She chanted the soft, comforting words inside her mind, and pulled on the rope until she was in a high squat. And then, an amazing thing happened.

A tiny golden star gathered at her brow, pulsing and glowing as she mustered every ounce of strength within her soul to push her baby into the world. She felt as if her body would turn inside out and explode. A final bloodcurdling scream echoed past the market, across the fields and hills, startling birds and deer, scattering bunnies and squirrels, quieting every living thing for leagues. Even in the town of Rockwall, a mysterious hush momentarily blanketed the dunborns and brightborns gathered there to celebrate Quickbane, the Day Without Time, the day between the end and beginning of the calendar year. The day when the veil is lifted between worlds and magic filters through the ethers, unchecked, waiting.

As the baby squirmed her way from a warm womb to the stiflingly hot tent, the shimmering star at her mother's brow gave a final pulse, shattered into a million bits of light and fell like fairy dust, twinkling briefly where it lay, and then vanished. The midwives had no time to marvel.

Agnes caught the baby, whose small body remained blue and lifeless, connected to her mother by a twisted umbilical cord wrapped tightly around her neck.

Beyond the tent, the good black stallion, Dragonfly, reared and whinnied loud and long, and was answered by a faraway shrieking neigh from a foaling mare. The stallion came down, stomping his great hooves into the earth, his breath intense and loud. For a moment, the stallion's powerful breath, chuffing in cadence with what was left of

Jasmine's own, was the only sound to be heard.

Outside, the world stopped. Bees stopped buzzing, flowers stopped blooming. Hammers stopped swinging, dogs stopped barking. Needles stopped darning. Children stopped playing, laughing, running. Water stopped boiling. Steam stopped rising. Even the clouds stopped drifting. The world held its breath, and listened with a hopeful ear.

Agnes quickly went to work untwisting the noose from the baby's small throat, panic rising as each eternal second passed. She rubbed the baby vigorously, folded in a soft towel. And then, at last, the tiniest sneeze followed by a single small cry. A sigh of relief, a cheer rang out across the Marketplace, and the world was alive again, rejoicing in the splendors of spring.

Inside the tent, the squatting young mother collapsed onto her back, and let her body and head fall into the comfort of familiar Andromedan silk cushions filled with the fragrant blossoms of her namesake flower. She knew that her own life was fast slipping away.

"It's a girl, Jasmine!" Agnes beamed. "You did it!"

"Let me hold her," croaked the weary mother.

Agnes gently laid the newborn, pulsing cord untwisted but not yet cut, skin still waxen, dark hair wet and matted to her small travel-bruised head, onto Jasmine's naked bosom. Young Myriam brought water to Jasmine's lips, but the exhausted woman rejected it. All she wanted was a moment with her child before she left the world without her.

The weight of the child was so slight, yet just weighty enough to be wildly comforting to the young mother. The baby's soft, confused squirming brought a peace to Jasmine's heart that she had never known. So small, so pink. She wanted nothing more than to protect this new life, and her heart instantly ached with the knowledge that she would not be able to protect her... from anything. Ever. Within seconds the baby's squirming lessened. She settled, curled herself into a quiet ball and then arched her tiny back to look at her mother. Puffy pink eyelids squeezed tight, blinked, just learning to open, and Jasmine's heart fluttered, even as her own body twitched and shuddered, and began to shut down.

A shaft of sunlight found its way into the tent, illuminating the scene in an ethereal way, passing through colorful scarves dancing in the breezeway, which cast washes of pink, lavender and tangerine light, and through faceted crystals, which scattered tiny, dancing rainbows everywhere. The midwives kneeled at Jasmine's side, one young, one old, as the new mother raised a trembling hand to cradle her baby's tiny head.

Finally, lashless eyelids parted, and the baby fixed her gaze upon her mother's face. Upon seeing those tiny eyes, impossibly lit like violet starbles in the sun, even in the colored shade of the tent, the two midwives let out a simultaneous gasp and hands flew to mouths in shock.

"Her eyes! They are as violet as the sunset!"

"She has Mystic eyes!"

And then, a circle of light etched itself into the baby's flesh, just above her heart, continuing in an intricate swirl of lines and curlicues until the bright and perfect image of a mariner's compass glowed like starfire upon her new skin, the needle spinning wildly at its center.

The eldest midwife sucked in a breath while the younger's eyes brimmed with tears.

"The Compass of Pyxis," breathed Myriam. "Her quickflame, look at it!" She shielded her eyes from the magic light.

"The Heart of Azimuth... Do you know what this means?" Agnes said in a hushed whisper with eyes wide as the sea.

"The legend is true," whispered the young mother, her voice rough as rocks dragging against sand. A shadow passed across her weary brow.

There was a pause as the gravity of this news sank into the hearts of the three women. None of them wanted to say it aloud. That the fate of not only their people, but their entire planet lay squarely in this tiny baby's tender hands. There was work to be done. So much this little baby would need to be prepared for.

"Aggie, call her Jesobel," said Jasmine weakly. She smiled sadly, "Please take care of her as your own. Teach her what she needs to know. Don't tell her about the compass until she's ready. Let her have a happy life, at least until then. Promise me you will?" Her voice was nearly gone, barely a scraping whisper.

"My dear Jasmine—what are you saying? You mustn't die!" cried Agnes, stroking Jasmine's slackened face.

"Oh, Jasmine, please don't leave us!" sobbed young Myriam, pale eyes glittering with tears, the glow of the baby's compass bathing the entire tent in Mystic light.

Jasmine traced the symbol on her daughter's chest with a soft finger, and it disappeared, as if she was erasing it, or tucking it away for another time. "Just take good care of my little Jessa, Aggie. She will be our Starkeeper now. Show her how to weave magic, and how to Keep our Realm. Hold her safe. Prepare her for this double-edged destiny. Please make sure she's strong enough…" Her child's future flashed before her eyes, and Jasmine gave a worried sigh. "I love you both. Myriam, you're the best friend a girl could have," she whispered. "Aggie, I owe you everything."

Aggie pursed her lips. "Jasmine, no! This isn't right. You mustn't leave us! You're just a child yourself! This can't be!" Agnes cradled her wilting apprentice in thin, birdlike arms, and begged Jasmine to fight for her life. The spry old Magic Weaver knew of no spell that could help restore Jasmine's health, though she tried in vain to think of one.

"Shhhh," hushed Jasmine, a finger to her lips, and the two midwives, eyes wild with terror, obeyed and said nothing more. Jasmine stroked her baby's small pink cheek with the back of her index finger, felt the softness of her silky dark hair beneath her open palm, and used the last of her energy to smile at her child. "You are the one we have been waiting for, my dear, sweet Jesobel. Shoshono fheelo, my magical little daughter. It won't be easy, but I know you can do it. You can lead our people back home. You can write a new ending to the legend and save Vale. You must."

Jasmine fumbled weakly with a golden ring until it slid from her finger. She placed it in the baby's curled palm, kissing her soft little knuckles for the first and only time.

And then, tiny Jesobel's young mother closed her exhausted eyes, never to open them again, as a pool of blood gathered beneath her and the wailing sobs of the grieving midwives filled the tent, their sounds of mourning stretching across the meadows and through the gate until every Mystic atom from the tent to Rockwall shimmered with their grief.

Across the valley in the Trading Arena, away from the rest of the herd in a bed of soft straw, a raven-black mare lay heavily on her side, weary from giving birth in the waxing twilight. She struggled to heave herself to standing, and immediately went to work licking at her wobbly colt's birth-slicked nose, just as the fireflies began their evening mating rituals, twinkling about like Vale-bound stars.

As the colt strained to remain upright and wobbled instinctively to his mother's side, a faraway neigh, deep and throaty like a salutation, floated in on the wind. The colt stiffened, and listened with small, pricked ears and a twitchy nose.

Young Finley Black watched the scene unfold. He approached the pair, but kept a respectful distance from the new mother and waited patiently to catch a glimpse of her foal. After a time, the mare turned around as if ready to show off her cleaned newborn, and the foal tottered into view, approaching the boy like an old friend. Fin sucked in a breath at the sight of the colt.

"Extraordinary," he said, stroking the colt's one white ear. A firefly landed on its dark brow and shined like a miniature star. Fin stepped back to admire the plucky fellow.

"Your coat looks as if it's been painted and sprinkled with the very stars above. I've never seen anything like it. You will be a remarkable stallion, little... Firefly."

Vallax

I licked my lips and blinked, squeezing my eyelids together. The mephitic tang of sulfur filled my mouth, burned my nostrils and stung my eyes.

Almost there.

The discomfort was intense for a moment. I was compressed, stretched, disassembled atom by atom. And then, with an electric crackle, my essence reassembled and I stood barefoot, stretching my cramped wings and legs—free at last from the compact, luminous prison where I had been trapped for an unknowable stretch of time.

I blinked again, my eyes unaccustomed to the gloriously dim room, and delighted in the feel of cool air upon my silky flesh. Sweet relief. I took an enormous breath, inhaling deeply to savor an onslaught of fascinating scents.

I gathered my senses, which weren't quite operating correctly just yet, and considered my situation. If Lesage, that idiot sorcerer, left even a particle-sized gap in my sigil, I'd find it and make a bloody ruin of him. And his ugly witch woman, too.

I paced a few circles, relishing the feel of a soft rug beneath my aching feet. Ahhh, a tremendous sensation. So much for a showy entrance; my limbs creaked like an old man's. My entire body felt stiffer than I thought possible. No matter, I had time. I had all the time I needed.

I dug my toes into the woolly carpet, drawing shapes in it with a taloned toe. I flexed my fingers and stretched my wings, then arched my back like a cat, ignoring my summoner for what I knew to be an annoying amount of time, waiting for my eyes to adjust properly to this new light.

As my surroundings came into focus, my mood cheered. At long last. I smacked my lips, inhaling the sweet scent of the sorcerer's blood. But I ignored him and looked around, delighting in the candlelit dimness of the... what was this place? Some sort of... castle... to which I was summoned. A welcome break from the bright golden nightmare cell from whence I came.

My summoner stood back, fear glittering in his eyes. Wait, no. Not fear. Surprise. Shock, really.

On second thought, there was fear. More than fear, actually. Absolute terror.

Curious.

And it was neither Lesage nor La Voisin.

Puzzling.

I gazed upon the young, frightened sorcerer who summoned me, and instantly deduced that he was an untrained nitwit. A child. An apprentice as best. He looked no more than seventeen. And that was being generous, based on his sorry attempt at some unbecoming configuration of facial hair.

"So, what do you want?" I yawned, a trifle bored and annoyed, pondering whether to shape-shift into something menacing for kicks. I tested my wings, thinking I would at least do some impressive acrobatics, but they were still so stiff and sore. My very plumes ached, and flap as I may, I couldn't get my feet more than a smidgen off the ground. Annoying.

I sniffed the air and froze. Something about this place, I finally noticed, was not quite right. I couldn't put my finger on what, exactly.

I shook out my hands and feet, jumped a little to warm up my bones. I ignored the young sorcerer, who stood speechless and couldn't seem to locate his words or shut his gaping guppy-mouth.

He glistened with nervous sweat. A look of utter disbelief contorted his face. Attractive.

From the shape of his face, I couldn't help but notice that I was obviously the first daemon he'd ever summoned.

Delightful. I enjoyed a good opportunity to amuse myself.

I folded my arms behind my head and struck a pose, did a little modeling for him. Let him enjoy my pubescent, milky skin. My smooth, cherubic cheeks. My seductive, oil-black eyes. I batted my feathery lashes. I flicked my pale wings, flexed them in little pulses. I gave him a little wink and grinned, letting him admire my multitude of blade-like teeth.

This unsettled the boy. He stumbled backward until he was pressed fearfully against an impressive colored-glass window overlooking a placid sea, painted pink with the light of the setting sun. I surmised by the view that the castle I currently inhabited was perched upon a stupendously high cliff.

The boy bored me with his saucer eyes and clueless disposition. No matter, the amateur's ignorance could only be to my advantage.

I scanned the floor for the circle of cobalt powder, which should have been keeping me in check. It was absent. For one brief moment, elation thrilled my spine, the boy's scent filled my nostrils, and I hungered. Not that I required food to survive. I hadn't eaten a morsel in who knew how long. I double-checked beneath my feet for my personal sigil, scolding myself for not noticing its absence sooner.

No sigil? What a ninny!

I rushed toward the foolish apprentice, hungry for freedom, hungry for blood, bent on shoving him through the rainbow glass to toy with him a bit on his deadly journey down, down, down, before making a snack of him once his body lay splayed and ruined on the jagged (I hoped) rocks below. I smirked, thinking of how I would pick my teeth with his splintered bones before hunting down Lesage and LaVoisin and popping their heads off for dessert.

I growled, let my teeth multiply in number, length and sharpness. I summoned wicked bolts of devilsflare to my ebony eyes until they flashed electric orange. I snarled and gnashed.

I could smell him, smell his sour fear-sweat. I could hear the blood pumping through his veins. I decided to shift completely. He would wet himself when he beheld my mighty Orphic presence!

I extended my wings. I was a little rusty—it had been a while—but I willed them into a new shape, exchanging my dainty white feathers for enormous, proper, leathery daemon wings. I set to work on my cherubic face, dementing it into a beastly form, delighting in the way the young sorcerer flattened himself into the leaded window and cowered like a frightened child at the sight of me.

As I worked at shifting into something ferocious, my impressively massive wings hit an unseen barrier mid-morph, mid-flap. My twisted face smashed into some invisible wall and I tipped backward, landing in a grotesque heap of half-shifted limbs and feathers.

Embarrassing.

I lay there, wondering. Could it be? Was I trapped inside the radius of some sort of *invisible* sigil?

Impossible!

I realized again that this entire place wasn't right at all. It smelled wrong. The sea smelled a little too salty. And it didn't even sound right. I tuned my ear, listened. It lacked a familiar pulsing beat between waves, crashing against the cliff below. There was a pulse, but the tempo was out of sync somehow, unfamiliar. The birdsong, I noticed, was different. What strange avian trills sounded outside the window! Everything felt just a little off, but I couldn't figure why. It almost smelled like the Mediterranean, but not quite.

Unsettling.

Perhaps it was me that was off from being trapped for so long. I scratched my chin, noting mid-muse that the wicked, pointy beard I had planned to add to my grotesque display had sprouted sideways from my face, finishing in an unbecoming curlicue.

Ridiculous.

I gathered myself back into my cherubic form, weary of the boy's simpering stares, and preened my slender, iridescent feathers. I then checked the circumference of the unseeable sigil like a Paris street mime, and ignored the incompetent sorcerer as I moved around the circle.

I sniffed the stony castle air a bit more.

Even the cool breeze sifting in through a cracked window smelled wrong. Alien spices drifted from some far-off stove, familiar, yet not. The crisp scent of autumn contained foreign aromas. Rotting blossoms I didn't recognize. Tangy decomposing leaves of both known and unknown trees. Even the faint scent of horse was not as it should be. There was something bright about this scent, something less musky and earthy than the horsey scent I was accustomed to abhorring.

I rolled my neck until it cracked, and took another deep breath, relaxing all the way to my toes.

I did, however, sense power here. The immense power that haunted me in my golden prison. It was near. I could feel it. It shimmered in the very molecules around me.

What was this place? Where was I?

I rolled my shoulders, swung my arms to loosen the stiff joints. I circled my ankles and breathed deeply. I felt energized.

Whatever this place was, wherever it was, I decided right then that I quite liked it.

I had a sudden inspiration, and reached toward this young

sorcerer with a strand of invisible devilsflare, cranking up the drama by stabbing a hooked talon maliciously toward the boy, delighting in the way my delicate, slender fingers struck fear into his tender, beating heart.

Unseen by his wide, rabbity eyes, my devilsflare crackled toward the boy, passing through the invisible sigil easily, like an electric tapeworm. I wasn't certain it would be so easy, but was pleasantly surprised by my good luck. I clipped an Orphic thread to him, twisted it around his heart and sent tendrils, like weeds, to take root in his fragile little mind, which I realized with glee was already fertile with a tendency toward dark thoughts and dastardly acts. Too easy!

I secured an anchor.

This invisible sigil wasn't half bad; a real sigil would never have let a thread through like that! I paced, hands on boyish hips, nodding my approval. It seemed fortune had smiled upon me, at long last.

From the corner of my eye, I saw the inept wizard step cautiously away from the window in a not-so-surprising plot twist, no longer flattened against it with terror. He edged closer and studied me, every movement vibrating the ethereal thread between us like a fly caught in a spider's web.

It wouldn't take long to crawl along the strand and possess him. Weeks, months perhaps, to stretch myself so thin, to get used to the feel of part of my essence stuck in that prison, part of it in the boy, without snapping back like an overstretched elastic band. Once I mostly possessed him, it was just a matter of time before I could use him to locate my golden prison and truly free myself by swapping places with the boy. Fitting him in that tiny prison would pose a challenge, but hey, I was up for it!

"Who are you?" He finally spoke. I couldn't determine whether he sounded braver than he felt or felt braver than he sounded. Stupid, I decided. He sounded infinitely more stupid than I'd figured. And he hadn't the foggiest clue who I was. Which, frankly, I found distasteful and rude.

"I am Vallax. Orphic Prince, Ruler of Daemons, known in some circles as the Dark Angel." I puffed myself up and then bent into a deep, mocking sort of bow, reaching my immense, feathery wings toward the high, domed ceiling. And then—I'd rather not have said it, but ancient, unbreakable Orphic rules are rules—I muttered, "At your service."

The boy heard this and a dark smile spread across his face. I noticed a sword in his left hand. He dragged it from behind his back, the tip scraping along the stone floor.

"Can you hex this sword?" he questioned, holding it out to me.

I nearly laughed aloud! Had I been drinking blood, it would have spewed from my nostrils!

What an idiotic question. What a dolt of a sorcerer. A puny hex? Even the dullest wizard wouldn't summon me for this! The boy was a complete and utter imbecile.

I flicked my eyes upward, annoyed that after being trapped for unknowable endlessness, cramped inside the most irritating golden orb, I was summoned to place a piddly hex on a dreary, boring sword by a novice child sorcerer, who knew not Whom He Had Summoned.

A dome of colored glass above my head featuring four galloping horses and some sort of crest interested me briefly.

"Why do you want me to hex this sword?" I asked with a sigh, breaking the rules, testing the limits of the invisible sigil.

The boy studied me, decided whether or not he could trust me. I encouraged him, silently, by sending a pulse down the Orphic thread. He was soon gossiping like a queen's handmaiden.

"My mother was denied a very special horse she wanted to purchase. And she decided if she couldn't have it, nobody could. She not only poisoned the horse she wanted, she poisoned the entire herd, the entire bloodline. And the woman who owned the horses was accidentally poisoned as well, and she was a Starkeeper, no less!

"The Mensan Council spared my mother's life against the Starkeeper's son's wishes, against the whole tiny population of Pegasus's wishes. 'A life for a hundred and eleven lives,' her son raged in court, but my father is a powerful man. My mother was released, with no real evidence to prove she had committed the crime, though I know it was her. Mother isn't exactly right in the head..." The amateur sorcerer became lost in his thoughts, barely registering my presence, and then his face tightened into a devilish shape.

"Anyway, I have lost one too many horse racing bets to her arrogant son, Helix, who now wears his dead mother's crown. I want to use this sword to slay my mother's finest horses, and frame the boy for the crime. Everyone will believe Helix was seeking revenge for his own mother's death and for the loss of his family's own herd. He'll be sent to prison, and then that gorgeous sister of his will take his crown, shaming him even further. He won't be able to bet against me at the races from prison, will he?" He had a smug look on his face that made him appear even more childish, which I didn't think possible.

"Hmmm, you want to slaughter your mother's horses?" It did sound delightfully messy to me, but not even close to messy enough. "But why not just slay the boy instead, if he irritates you so?" I had to ask the obvious question.

"Because I'm not a bloody murderer!" The young sorcerer's voice had a sudden wild edge to it. I saw a strange sort of rage flicker in his eyes.

"And my mother loves her stupid horses. More than she loves me. She deserves to live without them." He was spitting a little, all riled up. I liked it. I could work with that. After all, the distance between a horse murderer and a murderer is a mere two legs.

"So, can you hex the sword or not?" He was shaking, the quiver in his arm rattling the sword's tip on the stone floor. "I don't want the horses to suffer." His face glistened.

"Of course," I said, drawing my eyes downward in what I knew to be a slow and unnerving way. He edged backward, holding the sword out between finger and thumb like a filthy sock, all of his indignant rage melting back into sweaty fear.

Rules are rules, so I sent a showy streak of icy devilsflare to the blade, yawning all the while. Such an uncreative request. So utterly boring. I watched the devilsflare heat the blade, instilling within it enough Orphic magic to slay a thousand horses. I inhaled the light, tingly power that seemed to exist in the very atoms around me, both empowering me and sapping me of power simultaneously. Curious.

It amused me when the boy screamed from the shock and flipped the hexed sword against a stony wall. It clattered to the floor, crackling with a web of devilsflare threads. I suppressed a giggle at the look on his face, at the way he blew on his freshly scorched digits.

He stared at the sword on the floor, scalded thumb in his mouth, a look of awe slapped across his face. There was no way he was even a lowly sorcerer's apprentice. Who was this kid? And how did he manage to summon me? Daemon summoning was no small feat. Especially *this* daemon.

My answer came when the boy removed a golden bauble from his pocket, worrying it over and over in his palm.

He boldly stepped closer to me.

Studied me.

Decided I wasn't so scary after all.

Big mistake. But there was no reason to point that out now. Time was on my side. Time was always, ever on my side. I twanged the thread connecting us, and pushed Orphic magic into it, just enough to darken his cold heart a little bit more. Too much, too fast would kill him. One does not cultivate a murderous nature in mere minutes, after all.

The boy straightened his back, puffed out his chest and crept forward a few centimeters.

"Well done, Vallax," he congratulated me, a gesture which was both cocky and idiotic. Fascinating combo. If he had been close enough, I fear he would have attempted to slap me on the back as if we were old chums!

It would be like a carnival of wonders to occupy his twisted little mind. Puzzling, ridiculous wonders, anyway.

He regarded me, suddenly, as a prize, an asset. I regarded him as a scrawny plaything, which, clearly, with minimal effort on my part, would soon help me escape permanently from my little golden prison.

A wicked smile spread across his face. I smiled on the inside.

"And exactly who might *you* be?" I chewed at a snagged talon, feigning absolute boredom (he was my ticket to freedom, after all), and waited for his answer.

He lifted his chin and took another step closer, puffing out his chest.

Brazen. And none too bright.

"I am Ethan Rowan, Starkeeper-in-Waiting of Equuleus, Realm Thirty-Five of the Eighty-Eight Realms of Vale."

Interesting. I rifled through my memory for such a title, such a place, but my memory was a swirl of fragments and fog. Never mind that I had no idea where my golden cell was hidden, nor where in the vast universe I even was at this moment. I could be absolutely anywhere, in any galaxy. The sooner I learned of my prison's location—it had to be somewhat close by—and escaped from it, the sooner I could find my way back to France to punish those vile witches who trapped me in the first place. In the meantime, the power I sensed in this place called Vale intrigued me enough to postpone my plans for revenge and linger awhile.

The boy studied me. I enhanced my delicate features as his eyes passed across them, my black talons grew sharper, my wings more majestic. My grin, more toothsome and razor-like. My eyes, black as oil, seduced him with their fathomless depths.

Meanwhile, I considered his ordinariness. He was a handsome lad, I supposed, with a definite self-righteous air about him. His clothes, I noticed, were not the simple clothes of a sorcerer. A Starkeeper must be something royal, something regal in this strange new land, and not simply some sort of scientist who gazes pointlessly at the night sky. His accent, as he prattled on about my astounding awesomeness, sounded somewhat English. Somewhat, but maybe not quite.

But ah! Perhaps *that* explained the wrongness of this place! I was simply no longer in France! I had spent such a lengthy time in France (who could resist the pastries?) that I had forgotten completely that the Earth even hosted *other* countries. Could we be perched upon the Cliffs of Dover, inside the castle of a maddish boy, who fancies himself something special?

Again, I inhaled the air around me. No... no. This was not England. Vale, he said? Why hadn't I ever heard of it? Equuleus. Now *that* sounded familiar. I looked up at the domed glass, at the crest of this Equuleus. Ah, the crystal stars set in deep blue glass! The constellation Equuleus! Mystery solved. Except that it wasn't, really, was it? Equuleus, as far as I knew, did not include any habitable planets. Then where?

Whilst I puzzled over my whereabouts, too confounded to simply ask, the boy retrieved the hexed sword from the floor.

The devilsflare had calmed, the sword looked common again. He swished it through the air, spun circles with it, clearly comfortable wielding such a weapon. Gusts of the effervescent power of this place wafted across my face in the sword's wake.

"Well done, indeed, Vallax," he praised me again, his confidence erroneously expanding by the second.

"At your service, Horse Slayer." I gave him a wink and a new nickname. What a fool.

And then he sheathed the sword, and lifted the bauble in his hand towards me. He twisted a double-terminated crystal fixed to the center of it a click to the right, and finally stopped twisting after eleven more clicks, at which point I was instantly, violently transported back to my tiny golden prison, the Orphic strand I clipped to the boy stretching taught and painful, indicating a vast physical distance between the boy and my prison cell. It pained me to be unassembled and then compressed so tightly again after such a delicious moment of tasting a hint of freedom. The brightness pained my eyes. The gold impaired my abilities. The *tick, tick, tick* annoyed. The squeeze of the gold's Mystic glow on my Orphic essence irritated like a rusty razor dragged across tender flesh.

But I ignored it.

Locating my physical prison might not be as easy as I hoped, and yet it was the only way to truly free myself. At least I had a way to look for it now. If only I could find a map, a compass.

I smirked, feeling smug. That wannabe sorcerer had no idea what he'd set into motion. And it was best that he remained ignorant.

My vessel had been found. Now, to practice stretching myself along that thread until I could absorb his thoughts, his memories, seep my essence into him little by little without him even noticing. Take over his mind, bit by bit until I could use his body however I damn well pleased. It might be springtime before I could edit his horse-slaying revenge to a scheme far less mundane and wearisome. But I would add some real scandal to his plan. Murder in the first degree! The boy would slay his own parents!

CHAPTER 1

The white tower rose up behind young Ethan Rowan's city like an alabaster reef of pointed rooftops and jagged turrets, its pennants undulating like long red eels in a sea of bright blue sky. The watchmen stood atop the tower and along the great white wall, their armor flashing in the sun like a school of silver fish, keeping an eye on us Pyxies as we set up our shoppe stalls for the annual Quickbane Festival.

"Why don't you visit Myriam today and retrieve your new clothes, Jesobel? Those rags you insist on wearing are hardly befitting of a Royal Starkeeper," scolded Aggie.

"I'm hardly a Royal Starkeeper... yet." I sighed. "Must I?" I continued to hurriedly arrange tiny apothecary bottles on a tiered shelf by color.

Out of the corner of my eye, I watched a few stray white berries scatter to the green spring grass as Aggie's nimble old fingers wrapped purple ribbons around bundles of dried quickbane branches, and ignored her tightly pursed lips—her silent way of saying, "Yes, you must."

Instead, I delighted in the familiar sounds of hundreds of fellow Pyxians setting up their stalls all around us. Hammers tapped out rhythms, horses whinnied, children squealed, running amok with puppies on the outskirts of the marketplace, and people sang and laughed as they put up their tents and tidied their wagons, getting ready for our big weekend of commerce and trade.

A cool breeze caressed my cheek, lifting my hair from my sun-warmed neck in a soft way that made everything feel right in the world. So many of my people gathered all in one place. The Quickbane Festival felt like home. But there was a wagon I hadn't seen yet. Where was Glyn?

I took a deep breath, inhaling the clean, meadow-scented air, alive with the salty tang of the sea beyond the Cliffs of Rowan. Fragrant sweet clover and bright yellow dandelions and buttercups hummed with honeybees, blanketing the gentle hills all the way to the pale stone walls and to Rockwall's huge iron gate. How those people could stand to live trapped on the other side of a great wall and such an imposing gate was beyond me. Didn't they crave the freedom to roam from place to place? I would never understand middlings and their stationary lives.

"It's time for you to learn a secret about Quickbane, Jesobel." Aggie squinted against the late morning sun, hanging her bundles of branches and other herbs from the back of the stall, careful not to snag the fluttering silks which made a colorful makeshift wall to hide our camp.

"Quickbane is the day between worlds. The day between time, marking the transition from one year to the next." Her voice was twice as loud as it needed to be, a habit she formed when she became hard of hearing.

"Duh, everybody knows that, Aggie," I hollered, only half-listening. I stood on my tippy toes, peering over my godmother's halo of silver hair, all smushed down in the middle by her favorite scarf, and scanned the half-empty lanes for any sign of Glyn.

I sighed, disappointed, and checked the crate. So many little colored bottles left to unpack. Ugh. I felt antsy. Aggie had been smothering me with the most droll details about my upcoming responsibilities, over and over for the past few months.

"What everyone *doesn't* know, young Jesobel Vine," Aggie explained with a condescending edge to her voice, "is that for a short time during Quickbane, the veil is lifted between the ordinary world and the worlds beyond, both Mystic *and* Orphic."

"And?" I didn't see the point. *Why wasn't Glyn here yet?*

I checked the west gate, but the wagon rolling through it was not the wagon I was looking for. And way up on the hill, Steed Road was empty. Not a hint of dust kicking up. *He should be here by now.*

I caught Aggie giving me a hard look. "And *what,* Aggie?"

"And only when the full moon coincides with Quickbane, as it will this year for the first time in ages, are we able to summon the ghostmoths for the final hex in the Venoms Trivium. Our window is *very* small." I knew what she was really saying. She was really saying that I'd better not run off with Glyn and miss that lesson.

"Ghostmoths, right. Of course I'll be there, Aggie." But I couldn't help it. I just didn't really care about the Venoms Trivium all that much. Or about any of the annoying magic stuff I had to prove I could do in just a few days' time. Graduating from Apprentice to Magic Weaver only meant that I would be minutes away from embarking on a journey I didn't even want to make, to begin a life I didn't even want, a future I didn't even ask for. I didn't want to think about it. Not yet.

"You'd better be there, young lady. Missing that lesson is *not* an option."

My eyes were on the hill, scanning Steed Road again for Glyn's wagon, her words barely registering. "Aggie, may I please take a break and go for a quick ride?" I tried not to pout as I arranged the apothecary bottles in alphabetical order, sneaky shafts of bright spring sunlight illuminating the colored glass like the pretty starbles I collected as a kid.

Aggie shot me a look that could burn down seven realms, but I ignored it. I was getting pretty good at ignoring those looks, now that they'd become so frequent. I had a huge decision to make about Glyn before my life changed forever. I needed to find him. Why couldn't she understand that?

After making sure all the labels faced out, I stood back to admire our stall, a favorite among the middlings who would soon flood through the Rockwall gate and cross the meadow to make purchases from hundreds of exotic Pyxian shoppes. Aggie's Apothecary offered remedies for all sorts of ailments, and for the right customers, she'd even tell fortunes, never letting on that she was a true Magic Weaver. Our traditions were full of mystery and caused gossip amongst the middlings. We liked to keep them guessing.

"Did you put out the charms and enchantments? The love potions?"

"Yes, Aggie, they're all here."

"Are you certain you didn't mix up the bottles?" The novelty charms, enchantments and spells enhanced luck and love. They didn't have any real magic in them, but the middlings didn't know that. Aggie's authentic charms and spells were for Pyxians only.

"Yes, Aggie. All of the bottles with real magic are in the back." I sighed, frustrated that after all these years, she still didn't trust me to get it right.

The gold-leafed constellations adorning Aggie's wagon shone in the midday sun. The night sky and gold stars, along with intricately carved and painted flora and fauna all over the wagon, marked Aggie as both a Magic Weaver and a Healer among us Pyxies. Against a backdrop of rolling meadows, horse arenas and the glittering lake, our colorful wagon home was a sight so familiar, and yet, I realized suddenly, so fleeting.

An uneasy sensation settled in the back of my throat as I took in the landscape, as if my heart had crawled up there like a spider to lurk. I swallowed it down, not ready to accept that come Quickbane, I would be moving out of the only home I'd ever known and into my own new wagon, to begin the slightly terrifying journey to Saggita Harbor all alone. From there, I would sail to Corona Australis aboard the Queen's silver ship to claim my crown and serve my people as the next Starkeeper of Pyxis. I blinked, willing myself not to cry, and thought about Glyn instead. Beautiful Glyn with his sea-green eyes and honey-blond hair. Glyn and that warm, soft kiss we shared under the apple blossoms last autumn in Saggita. Glyn and his strong arms and easy smile.

Where was he?

I whistled for my horse, and excited nerves erupted in my belly as he sauntered around the wagon, tossing his head and nickering at me.

"Don't be gone long, Jesobel. It's already Thornsday." Aggie's scratchy, booming voice shifted to a spine-scraping whisper, which was ten times worse than her yelling.

"You've got a *tremendous* amount of work to do in the next three days." I hated when she looked at me like that, so intense that her halo of silver curls practically shivered with disdain.

"I know, I know. I'll finish that drawing of Firefly for Uncle Fin before the Igniting tonight. I promise," I lied, climbing easily onto Firefly's sturdy back and buckling my bow and quiver to my leather corset. His energy matched mine. We were both eager for a little adventure, but I combed bits of Firefly's long black and white mane with my fingers, waiting patiently for Aggie to scold me some more. I knew I was a terrible student; I knew that I wasn't even close to ready for any of my upcoming duties.

"Completing that drawing is the *least* of your worries right now, Jesobel. You need to graduate by Everday. And you still haven't packed a thing for your move!"

"I knowwwww," I whined, working at not rolling my eyes at her. Firefly's muscles tensed and twitched; he was as eager to gallop as I was.

"One hour. You get back here in *one hour*. Not a minute more!"

Aggie shook a bony finger at me and flicked her long scarf over her shoulder as if it were her hair, a motion which I'd come to know as the world's most intimidating gesture.

"Shosho, Firefly," I whispered to my horse, not wanting to stick around for any more of Aggie's wrath. He gathered his hindquarters beneath him and bolted, kicking up chunks of dirt and dandelions in our wake. I turned around to face Aggie, wind tangling Firefly's black and white mane with my own unruly hair as we thundered away. "An hour and a half!" I negotiated, unable to hide my joy at being free, and at moving way too fast for her to argue.

"Jesobel! Don't you dare be late! And get back here! Put your boots on before you go!" It was a habit of hers to demand I wear my boots. But I was born to be barefoot, and she knew I wasn't coming back for them.

I kept my eyes on Aggie for a second longer, grinning wide despite her anger. She shook her head at me in that deeply disappointed way that had become constant during the past year. I watched her unfurl the colorful pennants Uncle Fin would stop by later to affix atop the signpost along with the beautiful wooden shoppe sign he had carved for her.

The whole scene made me feel so nostalgic, I had to turn away and face the wind. I couldn't think about everything I would soon be leaving behind or I might come undone.

I forced myself to think only of Glyn's strong arms and soft lips. Which wasn't terribly difficult.

CHAPTER 2

*F*irefly's hooves pounded the sun-soaked grass, crushing innocent clovers and sending honeybees whirling as we galloped in a large arc around the marketplace. The tiny bells on my ankles tinkled in cadence with every strong beat, my soft old skirts whipping across my legs in the most luscious way, while my eye was on constant lookout for an aging lemon-yellow wagon with pale blue and white bubbles carved into its sides. The whole world smelled so fresh and divine, I just wanted to keep on riding and never go back.

I circled Firefly around the outskirts of the marketplace, scanning wagon after colorful wagon, stall after brightly decorated stall in search of Zola's Soap Shoppe, but it was clear that Glyn and his mother had yet to arrive. My heart sank. I made Aggie show up four days early this year because Glyn and Zola were usually among the first wave of wagons arriving on Mossday. And now it was already Thornsday! Three and a half days I'd been waiting. Three and a half days I'd been distracted by thoughts of Glyn's tender kiss while Aggie lectured me about my stupid destiny during breakfast, lunch and supper, and every minute in between. And now I just felt tortured that he wasn't here.

We crossed past the marketplace and cantered up the sloping meadow toward the small paddock where Liam, Aunt Myriam's father, kept his herd of tall sport horses, a Festival favorite among the wealthy brightborn middlings.

"Hello, Liam!" I waved, steering Firefly toward the fence.

"Jessa! Good to see you, darlin'! How's that wild stallion of yours?" Liam swung himself onto a post and took a seat, while a handful of horses pushed their noses over his shoulder to greet Firefly. "It's always a pleasure to see old Dragonfly's boy. Not sure I'll ever get used to his wild coloring," he said, admiring Firefly's flashy black and white coat. "Especially those stars on his black spots. I'll be a shadow sprite's supper if those aren't actual constellations!"

"Yeah, Aggie knows which ones they are. I don't remember, though." I grinned. "Except for this one." I reached around Firefly's thick neck and tried to pat his muscled chest. "That's Pyxis!"

"You don't say? Well, I'm not surprised. There's always been something different about that horse. Something special. Maybe it's that wild Mystic eye that matches yours so perfectly."

"Maybe," I laughed, patting Firefly's neck. "So, what's the news? Any good gossip on the road?" Liam was one of those people who had an ear for travelers' tales. Something about moving along the roads with a herd of unbelievably beautiful and well-behaved horses made people trust him in ways that the rest of our people would never experience. They also tended to look out for him, warning him if horse bandits were near.

"Oh, there were whisperings along the River Equine, stories about Ethan Rowan, that new young Starkeeper and his gambling ways. From what I heard, the river folk agree that the other twin, the level-headed one, would make a more sensible Starkeeper. Shame about their parents, murdered like that. And with a hexed sword! It's a wonder the Festival is still happening, what with the funeral just last Sorrelday."

"Really sad," I agreed, not wanting to think on it too much. "I heard that Ethan Rowan has a thing for horses," I said, absently braiding a chunk of Firefly's long mane.

"Indeed. Better not let that young Starkeeper see this beast of yours," he joked, giving Firefly a pat on the nose, but a shiver threaded up my spine.

Liam continued, "Ethan's mother, Ellsa, may the Mystic weave her spirit"–he scribbled the Mystic sigil in the air with his finger–"had a collection of the finest horses from around the globe."

He paused thoughtfully, as if remembering something from long ago. "You know, she weren't right in the head, that woman. I knew it last time she bought a horse from me. Somethin' was just off. If I didn't know her stable boys so well, I wouldn't have ever sold her a horse." Liam shook his head sadly, scratching the nose of a blagdon mare whose big head rested in his lap. His way with horses was something to behold.

"So do you think it's true that she poisoned a whole herd of horses up north somewhere last autumn?" I had heard this tale myself, when we passed through a small Pyxie village in Saggita. "And a Starkeeper, too?" I couldn't believe it. Things like this didn't happen in hardly any of the Realms of Vale. Certainly not on our continent. Ophiucus and Lacerta, maybe. All those dry, desert realms full of prickly creatures, plants and people. Never here.

"Aye, that's what they're sayin' but I don't know if I believe that or not. I do know that herd of horses was Starkeeper Airheart's pride and joy. Never did lay eyes on one o' her beasts myself. Word is she was poisoned right along with them marvelous creatures o' hers, may the Mystic weave her spirit," said Liam, finger-drawing the spiral sigil in the air again.

"So nobody really knows for sure who poisoned Starkeeper Airheart and her horses? Does anyone know who killed Ellsa and Ewan Rowan?" I shuddered at the thought of so much blood. "Or why?"

"They don't know who done it yet, last I heard. Or why. Was only a few days ago, after all. That Rowan boy took up his crown fast, considering the blood of his parents has barely had time to dry."

"So much death…" I was horrified to hear such tales. I felt uneasy. Two Starkeepers had lost their lives in just a few months' time, and nobody knew why. I was about to become a Starkeeper myself. "How could anyone do something so awful? And all those horses poisoned, too?"

"I don't know, darlin', I don't know. It certainly makes my particular trade feel a little less comfortable, if you know what I mean." I did know what he meant. I knew exactly what he meant. I shuddered, hugging myself with a sudden chill. As if I didn't already have enough reasons for not wanting to be the Starkeeper of Pyxis.

"I sure hope Ethan Rowan rises to the responsibility he's been given. Quite the reputation, that young man. Many people are worried he's neither prepared nor fit for such a position of power just yet. Or maybe ever."

Unfortunately, I could relate. I let out a big sigh, frustrated by how little time I had left to just be myself before I accepted responsibilities I didn't feel the slightest bit equipped to take on. Liam jumped down on the paddock side of the fence, his mares nosing his pockets for treats. I needed to find Glyn.

"You haven't seen Zola's wagon, have you?" I asked.

"I did pass Glyn and Zola a week or so back. I imagine they'll be along in a day or so." He winked. My heart sank.

"Good to see you, Liam." I waved. "I guess I'm off to shoot some arrows at the archery range." I had to do something to get my mind off all this.

CHAPTER 3

We veered south, my bones thumping comfortably with the beat of Firefly's hooves on the grass as we galloped along the great white stone wall, which flanked the steepest, highest cliffs in all of Vale. The huge, smooth stones snaked along the craggy cliff top, following the curves, hills and valleys as far as the eye could see. The salty sea air added a heady tang to the crisp, clean breeze which meandered south from the snow-capped Percherons, ushering rabbles of butterflies in every hue in its wake. Every hoof beat shook a little darkness from my mood; every breath of fresh air soothed me a tiny bit more.

Just past Bat Rock, I looped right, heading up the other side of the lake and back towards the small grove of trees above the marketplace, leaving Liam's unsettling stories behind. The equestrian archery range overlooked the gentle valley with a stunning view of Rockwall and Rowan Tower. I took in the sweeping landscape. Beyond the gate, the dunborns and brightborns were barely ants from way up here, already enjoying the third day of the Festival with games of skill, horse races, dog races and puppet shows. What else they did until Everday was a mystery to us Pyxies. We weren't allowed beyond the Rockwall gate, nor were we invited to enjoy any of their festivities. But we were used to it, and made our own fun. A sense of melancholy crept into my heart as I realized again that this would be the last time I would be just plain old Jesobel at a plain old Quickbane Festival. Next year, I would be a Royal Starkeeper. And my duties might put me on the other side of the world, tending to a scattering of my people on another continent altogether, or even somewhere in the middle of the Silver Sea. I shuddered at the thought. And the disturbing thoughts that came with it.

The archery targets had been given a fresh coat of paint; they stood out bright against the dark tree trunks. I urged Firefly into action. Dodging trees and hay bales, Firefly threaded through the course until my quiver was empty, each arrow sinking into its target with a satisfying *shoonk*.

"Firefly," I whispered, yanking the last arrow out of its target and returning it to my quiver, "I don't know how I'm going to live without Glyn." I slid off his back and sat on a rock, tossing my equipment at my feet.

Firefly snorted and meandered a few steps to find a juicy patch of clover, his ear turned toward my voice.

Plucking a glassflower from a little cluster near my toes, I began to pop off the petals one by one.

"I'm going to make a terrible Starkeeper, Firefly," I explained to my horse. "And I honestly don't know if I'll even graduate to Magic Weaver in time. You've seen my magic! It's out of control. How will I learn three powerful hexes by my birthday without destroying everything within a hundred-league radius?" Firefly nickered. "Sorry, *our* birthday. That's only four days from now!"

When I bent to grab another glassflower, telling myself I wouldn't dare play *he loves me, he loves me not* to see if Glyn and I could find a way to be together, despite the stupid tradition dictating otherwise, a sparkle in the grass caught my eye. I leaned farther, stretching to grab it.

"Ouch!" A jeweled pin stuck into my palm. I pulled it out, sucked on the bloody spot and examined my prize.

It was a kite-shaped amulet of some sort. A drop of blood slid down the golden pin and settled into a groove at its base as I hooked the clasp closed. I tried to wipe it off, but the blood vanished into a crack like a sponge absorbing water. Strange.

The amulet looked expensive. I held the edge of the metal and turned it over, looking for a clue about its owner. I had never seen anything like it. The designs etched into the back were certainly not Pyxian, or even Casseopiean. They looked completely foreign.

There was something dark about the symbols, something dangerous that set my quickflame on edge. I shivered, suddenly aware of the cold, mineral scent of the rock I sat on. The grass cooled beneath my bare feet, as if a winter frost had seeped up from its roots.

I flipped the amulet over and inspected a double-terminated crystal held in place by a band of gold around its center. The translucent stone swirled inside with the color of shadows and blood. I shivered, a rimy chill gripping me like a cold embrace.

Marks etched around the golden edges of the brooch indicated numbers. The number at the top read 12, and one end of the crystal pointed to it.

Without thinking, I twisted the stone, my teeth chattering with a sudden shiver. The stone clicked and settled into a groove at the next marker. I twisted it again and again, until it had clicked eleven times. It reminded me of a clock, but why did it only go to twelve? And why was it flat? I twisted it again. When the crystal returned to its starting position, it shuddered violently in my hand.

It began to buzz, and deep, smoky shadows roiled ominously inside the pale stone. A dark, red-orange glow emanated from within it and there was an ear-piercing crackle as a ferocious jolt tore through my quickflame like lightning, racing through my bones until I was paralyzed, unable to move a muscle, both cold and hot all at once.

My tiny spark fairies burst from the portal near my chest in a frenzied line, whipping out and away from me, shrieking in pain, their little wings beating violently. I couldn't move to help them; I couldn't even scream for help. I just sat there like a silent statue, my quickflame firing off in wild bursts as if it were trying to escape from me, as if it were in pain.

I watched Liliet and my entire force of illumins flutter haphazardly toward Firefly, who had wandered away, chasing after sweet clover and drooling like a beast because of it.

There was an icy, burning sensation above my sternum, tracing a pattern as if someone were carving my skin with a frozen ice pick. My body felt stuck in time. I managed to bring a hand to my chest and feel what was happening there. A violet flare, glowing hot with quickflame, yet burning with a chilling coldness that felt like the deepest dread and fear and sorrow, continued to etch some sort of sigil into my flesh. The pain was outrageous, but my screams were trapped, unable to escape my lips.

When the symbol was complete, a heavy pulling sensation tugged downward through my spine into the rock beneath me, and a deep sense of misery washed over my spirit, as if I were mourning the loss of a hundred thousand souls. The deep heartache was unbearable.

I peered downward at the shape scorching my chest, violet blades of quickflame licking outward like a beacon. There, etched below my collarbones, ablaze with quickflame brighter than anything I'd ever seen, was a compass; the needle spinning madly, wildly.

"Aren't you a lovely little thing?" The smooth voice came from behind me. Fear blossomed at the base of my skull and snaked down my spine, hollow and uneasy.

I stood, the paralysis gone, a feeling of ice shattering and falling away as I whirled around. The compass on my chest flashed, violet light stabbed every which way, and I felt like a firework gone wrong. My head spun and my footing was unsteady.

The creature standing before me leaned against a sapling and chewed absently at a long black talon. He was nude, wearing only a covering of black leather which hung about his slender hips. His skin was the color of moonlight, pale and bluish. He had a shock of unruly hair as black as a starless night and large, fathomless eyes dark as volcanic rock set in a face both eerie and beautiful. Sprouting from his shoulder blades were the wings of a heron, with iridescent white feathers both soft and downy, and razor sharp. The Orphic energy emanating from him was more intense than anything I'd ever experienced. I shivered where I stood, sick with fear. I wrapped my arms around myself, the amulet digging into my fingers and palm, and tried to hide the magic shooting from my chest.

"Who are you?" I croaked, stepping away from him.

"What's all this?" He said, circling a hooked claw in the air to indicate the light show escaping from beneath my arms. Long, feathery eyelashes framed those creepy black eyes, and they fluttered as he watched the magic flaring from the compass. A wry smile moved the corners of his mouth upward a little. "I like it!" He grinned. A thousand needle-sharp teeth filled the crescent shape made by his parting lips. I shuddered, remembering the shadow sprites in Archer's Forest, their teeth so very similar.

The winged boy paced circles around the tree, flexing his wings and fingers, as if pondering some great mystery, or concocting some sort of plan.

"Who... who are you?" I asked again. "What do you want?" I could barely stand up straight. Magic whirled from the compass, pushing me this way and that. I envied the boy's sapling to lean on. I hoisted a foot upon the rock to steady myself.

He sighed as if bored beyond measure and bent into a dramatic bow with a flourishing hand gesture. "I am Vallax, Orphic Prince, Ruler of Daemons. Some call me the Dark Angel." He stood, stretching his jagged wings upward in a showy way, and curtsied. And then I heard him mumble, "At your service."

"At my service?" I stumbled around, the spinning needle knocking me off balance. I felt drunk and gave the rock a dirty look for failing to hold me still.

"Indeed," he said, yawning. "Say, why don't you tell me about that fascinating sigil lighting up your chest."

Vallax focused on the sapling, whose papery bark he used to sharpen the edge of a talon. "Is that a compass?" A hint of a smile passed across his pale lips, sparkled in his black eyes.

A cold and sinister flood of energy seeped into my hand and shot up my arm. It strangled my magic, yet at the same time gave me a wild surge of power—for a brief second I was limitless, my quickflame radiating from me with immense force. It was intoxicating. I felt I could do every spell Aggie had ever attempted to teach me and then some, but it was all wrong. Way too much devilsflare. I pushed back with my quickflame, guiding the dark magic back down my arm, out. Out into the amulet in my hand.

"Did you like that little blast of extra power? Want some more?" The winged boy leaned forward, suddenly attentive, grinning, pointing at me with a hooked claw.

Another surge blasted up my arm. "No! Please, stop!" The needle spun out of control, waves of nausea surged in my stomach like a tempestuous sea. I stumbled, dizzy and delirious. I clapped a hand over my chest, tried to calm the needle, hide the bright light bursting from my sternum. "Please, please stop!" I begged, as the compass grew icy cold with devilsflare.

Vallax giggled as I struggled to remain upright, to use my quickflame to fight back. My left palm ached. I realized my fingers were frozen around the amulet. I wanted to toss it away, but I couldn't let go of it. The needle on the compass in my chest spun faster and faster, its scorching burn nearly unbearable as it generated powerful magic steeped in darkness. Devilsflare moved through me like poison.

"Firefly… Liliet." I bent over, steadying myself with one hand on my knee and slid my eyes in the direction of my Mystic fairies who writhed in pain on the back of my horse with every eruption of devilsflare in my quickflame.

Everything looked off-kilter and warped. The gyrating needle whirred around and around on my chest, each rotation more dizzying than the last. My stomach churned and a sickening pressure built at the back of my throat. The devilsflare burned in my very veins. I had to do something or I felt like I might die.

Firefly growled and chuffed, lowering his head as he approached, finally noticing my sorry state. I slid my hand under his forelock and pushed my palm into his soft forehead to steady myself. Blades of light escaped through my fingers. Firefly's star glowed with Mystic magic, and then all of the stars on his coat lit up until he sparkled like the night sky. The needle slowed. It wiggled back and forth, as if looking for a good place to stop. The bright light of it finally calmed to a more comfortable, dull glow. Warmth spread from my horse to my hand and blanketed me in steady quickflame. The painful devilsflare retreated back into the amulet, slinking away like a frightened snake. I leaned into my horse, barely strong enough to hold myself up.

"Fascinating!" said Vallax, his black eyes wide with delight.

"What do you want?" I begged, mildly better with that devilsflare out of my system.

"The question, my lovely, is what do *you* want?" The creature folded his hands and took on an angelic pose, eyes wide and inquisitive. Waiting.

The question had an unexpected impact. Had anyone ever asked me what I wanted? No! Nobody ever asked me if I wanted to be a Magic Weaver. Nobody ever asked me if I actually *wanted* to be the Starkeeper of our people. Nobody asked me if I could stand to live without Glyn, to know that he would marry another maiden soon after I was gone! Heat filled my cheeks, fury for sixteen years of being treated unfairly, told what to do, of never once being asked what I wanted. A sense of indignation spread through every particle of my being so fast that words cascaded from my mouth without any consideration whatsoever.

"Freedom. That's what I want. That's all I've ever wanted!"

"Then you and I aren't so very different." Vallax grinned, his needle teeth glinting in the sun. A stab of regret pierced my mind before he spoke the next words. "You shall have your freedom, my lovely. And in turn, I shall have mine." His grin faded slowly and his eyes grew cool and emotionless. Everything drained from my body, like my very life was being sucked from me. For a brief millisecond, I was relieved. I was dying, and it was okay. And then Firefly screamed in my ear, jostled me with the bridge of his nose and my spark fairies gathered, whipping around me like a tornado of light, pushing quickflame into my body, into my spirit. The sensation was fizzy, bubbly, I was elated and was able to join them, summon Mystic magic from the grass, the trees, the butterflies. Power coursed through me, but it wasn't like the Orphic power, it felt clean and light. It filled me, searching every atom for darkness and chased that darkness back down my arm and into the amulet. The amulet that was connected to Vallax, I realized.

I cast my eyes downward, at the metal bauble humming icily in my palm, my fingers still frozen stiff around it. I knew, somehow, that if I could just turn that crystal...

In an instant, Liliet flew toward me. She twisted the crystal with all her might, her tiny, pregnant body pressed against its length, my heart swelling with love at her fierce loyalty to me. I looked at Vallax, feeling triumphant.

His eyes shifted with the slightest hint of surprise, before settling on a look of indifference. "It's okay, my lovely. We shall meet again."

"Not if I can help it!" I said, sending a surge of quickflame to Liliet's small body.

Her mate soon joined her, and then there were many illumins, all working together to move the crystal a notch to the right, tiny wings fluttering at atomic speeds. The glow of their Mystic bodies dimmed when they touched the Orphic crystal. It sapped their strength, but they didn't give up. I sent them more magic. I drew it from all around me, from the rocks and trees, and wove it like so many golden threads and pushed it to my fairies.

When the crystal finally clicked into place, my tiny heroes collapsed in a heap on my hand.

"Toodle-oo." Vallax waved. "I honestly can't believe my luck." He grinned, as his body disassembled into a mass of shivering atoms, which were sucked like a vortex into the amulet with such force that I was slammed to the ground. All of my quickflame vanished instantly, leaving my fairies and me drained. They lay limp and exhausted, relief sagging their small faces.

"Go back to the Mystic, Liliet. You all need to recharge," I croaked. I held my hand to my heart, and they stumbled into the portal, vanishing with a series of ticklish clicks and pops.

I twisted around and vomited violently into the patch of glassflowers, my body quaking in the aftermath of holding all of that quickflame and devilsflare inside of me.

When I wobbled to standing, Firefly was there to catch me with his great muzzle.

"What was that all about?" I coughed, and leaned into Firefly's soft coat, looping an arm around his neck to steady myself. I opened my palm and eyed the amulet suspiciously, unsure what to do with it, and absently ran my fingers across my chest, tracing the shape of the compass, but it was no longer there.

"Firefly, it's gone!" I could feel its presence, like a phantom burn, but the compass had vanished without a trace. How would I explain any of this to Aggie without some sort of proof? Firefly nickered and sidled up to me, meaning for me to hop on. I was weak, but I managed to climb aboard, the amulet still clutched in my fist.

"There is something desperately wrong with this trinket and that creepy Vallax lurking inside of it. Aggie will know what to do," I told Firefly. But fear took root in my belly and began to gnaw at me in a nervous, uncomfortable way. I wasn't one hundred percent certain Aggie would be helpful. And I was about ninety-nine percent certain she would be furious with me for not being more careful with that amulet.

There was, after all, an entire moon of lessons spent on amulet safety. Two entire weeks on exactly what NOT to do with an unfamiliar amulet. A whole moon of lessons in which, clearly, I had learned nothing whatsoever.

Halfway down the hill, I realized the stark truth.

"Aggie's going to kill me if I tell her about this, Firefly."

CHAPTER 4

After a quick nap to recover, I scrubbed the dishes and did the fifty million other non-magical chores Aggie forced me do before the Igniting, never finding an appropriate moment to show her the amulet and tell her about meeting the so-called Orphic Prince. Not that I was in a hurry to get into heaps of trouble. I at least wanted to see Glyn first.

I pulled on one of my nicest skirts and favorite leather corset, which apparently were not nice enough to receive approval from Aggie.

"It's disgraceful, Jesobel! You are to be our Starkeeper," she scoffed, shoving a new blouse in my face. "At least put this on and we'll just hope it draws attention away from your raggedy old skirts. Myriam says your Coronation outfit isn't quite ready yet, or you better believe you'd be wearing it right now!" She attacked my head with a brush and tried to tame my hair into something less wild, and failed. The second she finished, I darted toward the door.

"Can I go now? Please?" I whined, testing her patience.

She punched her fists into her hips and stared me down like a cantankerous jailer, lips pursed so tight I thought her face might turn inside out. "Didn't you forget something?" She eyed me with a perilous glare. A chill washed over me, and I knew I'd really blown it.

I mentally catalogued everything she'd been harping on me

to remember for the Igniting, my stomach doing uneasy flips as each eternal second passed under her scrutiny, and I couldn't come up with whatever it was I was forgetting. And then it hit me, thank Ariah!

"Oh, right! My quickbane wreath." I forced a half-hearted laugh. She found no humor in my oversight. She crammed the wreath onto my head, affixing it with a slew of hairpins without bothering to be gentle about it. I tried not to flinch.

"There," she announced, jamming the last pin into my scalp. I fought the desire to check it for blood.

"*Now* can I go? *May* I... go," I corrected myself. I ached to get out of there. She scanned me from head to toe, clearly unsatisfied with the whole ensemble, but nodded almost imperceptibly, disgust curling her lips into a visible sneer.

"Do not be late for the Igniting of the Quickfire, Jesobel. Do not disappoint me." Her tone was so intense that I almost withered under its power.

"I'm serious," she reminded me, as if I couldn't tell. I grabbed my boots and shoved my feet in them, just to please her enough to take the edge off a little.

"Look! Boots!" I grinned, fishing for a smile. "I'll be there at moonrise, I promise." I kissed her stony cheek and skipped out the door, grabbing an apple from the hanging basket, and vanished into the shadows of the night.

"Jesobel, don't you dare be late!"

CHAPTER 5

I ignored Aggie's shouts and ran down the alley between shoppes until I was close enough to the great fire pit, which stood ready for me to ignite. I ducked behind a tinker's wagon, positioning myself so that I could see the gathering of people around the pyre without being noticed. I wanted to be close enough to listen, to smell the horses and hay and fading cookfire smoke—the spices and perfumes that made the Quickbane Festival feel like home in a way no other place on Vale did.

I wanted to wait for Glyn to arrive, to have him by my side during my first official Igniting. I wasn't ready to brave all of the attention that came with being the Royal Starkeeper-in-Waiting. Especially since most of the attention would be negative at best. Hardly anyone but Glyn and Uncle Finley believed I was remotely cut out for this unwelcome destiny.

I dug a piece of parchment from my skirt pocket, along with a stub of pencil, which sat nestled near that disturbing crystal amulet—which gave me a jolt of guilt as my hand brushed against it. I promised myself I would tell Aggie later, after I had a chance to spend time with Glyn.

Using a stray wagon stool as a desk, I squatted down and struggled with the millionth unflattering sketch of my horse; scribbling, blending and erasing to the merriment of flutes, fiddles, clapping and singing. I wasn't in the mood for any of it. I needed time before I braved that crowd. And I really, really needed to finish drawing Firefly for my new wagon, or else I would be the worst, laziest Starkeeper-in-Waiting to ever walk the planet. Which was already the general buzz about me.

Uncle Fin snuck up behind me and jammed two fingers into my ribcage. I squealed and fell over, taking the tiny desk with me, too lazy to get up right away. I just lay there in a heap, head in the grass, gripping my pencil, stuck in a weird upside-down moment. I stared at the sky, at the moons and stars poking through the twilight. The stars winked back at me and I couldn't help but feel that they were judging me, too—*she's got no business being the Royal Starkeeper to those people. She's too careless, too young, too wild.* Everyone knew it was true. Nobody more than myself.

"Hey, is that for me? Did you finally finish designing your talisman? I'm running out of time to carve that above your wagon door, young lady! Give us a look." Fin nudged me with a foot, laughing deep and hearty.

"No." I frowned at my hideous drawing, squirreled it away into my pocket before he could see it, inched my way up to a sitting position, and then decided against it and flopped back into the clover.

"Fine. But you'd better have it done soon. Guess what? I have news for you. I visited the Nyxie Post cove back in Steward's Draft. A bottle arrived from Starkeeper Yarrow. Looks like this is getting real, Jessa! Pretty exciting stuff, eh?"

"Not really." I went boneless and sank deeper into the clover with a sigh, wishing I could vanish without ever reading the message.

"Sure it is! Come on, you've been training your whole life for this." Fin offered me a hand up. I glared at it, and when it didn't go away, I reluctantly took it. He pulled me to my feet, pushing a corked glass bottle with a little scroll sealed inside toward me.

"What's it say?" asked Fin, far too interested. "Do you think it's the

Starkeeper's Secret?"

I stared at the wax seal, at the sigil that Starkeeper Yarrow had chosen for me. It was a compass. I shuddered, an itch crawling beneath my collarbone. I felt suddenly woozy, but couldn't quite figure out why.

"I don't know. I hope not."

"Well, what else could it be? Good tidings for a successful Igniting? I highly doubt it." Fin laughed. His wide, easy grin did nothing to ease the skein of nerves knitting itself into a knot in my stomach. "You're about to learn the Secret. The only existing clue about the location of our lost realm. You're the Keeper now, Jessa!" Fin said, with an enthusiasm in his voice that I couldn't relate to. He gave my arm a friendly punch.

"Ow," I said, but didn't mean it. A shiny gold ribbon embedded in the violet beeswax crossed over itself beneath the stamped sigil, the ends sticking out just enough to pull. I hesitated, not ready for any of this. Of course the scroll contained the secret. Starkeeper Yarrow didn't send nyxiegrams for no good reason, and Aggie had warned me that the secret would arrive whenever I was ready. But I certainly *wasn't* ready! I didn't think I'd *ever* be ready.

"She's putting an awful lot of faith in me, giving me the secret before I even graduate to Magic Weaver!" I scowled and flicked my eyes across the bustling marketplace toward the boys piling moon tree logs onto the pyre, along with some hawthorn boughs for Thornsday.

I scanned the circle for Glyn out of habit, in search of his turquoise violin, which was usually so easy to spot. By the time my eyes made it back to Fin's face, he was glowering at me.

"What if I fail the Venoms Trivium?" I fiddled with the ribbon, afraid to pull it. Once I lay eyes on the Secret, it would be removed from Starkeeper Yarrow's memory, and only exist in my own. It had been passed from Starkeeper to Starkeeper for centuries this way. I felt a little sick. "What if I don't want to Keep the Secret?"

"Jesobel! Imagine if you hadn't come along in time! What if Starkeeper Yarrow, Ariah forbid, had *died* before you were born? She's ancient! It easily could have happened. Then the Secret would have perished! And then the Lost Realm would truly be gone. Forever! But you, young lady, were born. Just. In. Time." He poked my shoulder with each word, and then hooped my nose.

I squirmed. It wasn't my fault somebody centuries ago lost our entire realm, or that now there was some magical secret about its possible location that only I would soon possess. How could anyone even do that? Lose an entire realm? And who cared, anyway? It wasn't like our people even wanted to go there. Pyxians travel. It's what we do. We don't stay in one place for more than a moon or two. Ever. I didn't care where that stupid Lost Realm was. Nobody did. It was a pointless Secret to be forced to Keep.

"How is anyone certain that I'm the true Starkeeper-in-Waiting anyway, Fin?" I beheaded a dandelion with my toe, the tinkle of my ankle bells like a miniature death knell. "What if I'm not really cut out to be our Starkeeper?" I thought about this a lot. Every day, in fact. Aggie was constantly frustrated by my lack of focus during my studies. I wasn't the only one who doubted my skill to take on such a huge responsibility…

Fin laughed in my face. "Oh, right, because Mystic-eyed Quickbane babies are born every single year, right? There are just tons of possible Starkeepers-in-Waiting to choose from!" He scoffed at me. "Of course it's *you*. Who else could it possibly be, Jessa? Don't be ridiculous! You're a rare gem, Jesobel Vine. Your people need you."

Maybe he had a point, but I didn't want all that responsibility. "I don't know, Fin."

"You can do this, Jessa. It's your destiny. The Secret needs a Keeper, and you're it, like it or not. You're going to be our Starkeeper. You're just going to have to accept your fate. You've got quickflame running through your veins."

But I didn't want quickflame running through my veins. I just wanted to be a regular Pyxie maiden. I just wanted to live a happy life with Glyn and my faithful Firefly—the best horse a girl could ever ask for. I just wanted to be free to live my life my way.

I squeezed my eyes until tears slipped down my cheeks, inhaling a tiny sob. The ghost of Glyn's kiss shimmered on my lips, where it had lingered since last autumn. *Why hadn't I kissed him back just a little bit more?* I scanned the crowd for his bright fiddle. *Because Starkeepers don't marry,* I reminded myself. *Because you love Glyn too much to ask him to sacrifice everything for you.* I felt like kicking something. Instead, I opened my fat mouth without really thinking.

"Fin, what would you say if I told you that I…" I took a deep breath and exhaled the words into the ground, barely a whisper, afraid to look at him. Afraid to admit the truth out loud. "That I don't want to be our Starkeeper?"

Aggie would hex me for saying such things. I toyed with the ribbon on the nyxiegram. I didn't want to open it. My eyes welled with tears.

Fin lifted my chin with a rough, work-worn finger and wiped a tear from my cheek. "Oh, Jessa, don't say that, you don't really mea–"

I didn't let him finish. Before I had the sense to bite my tongue, I pushed his hand away and blurted the worst thing I ever could have said, "Well, you know what? I *don't.* I don't want to be our Starkeeper, Fin. *I don't.* I'm not ready. I don't think I'll *ever* be ready!" I shoved the nyxigram bottle into his hands like it was filled with poison.

Fin went silent. I could feel his disappointment, his disgust in me, in my confession, trembling, palpable between us. I regretted my words, but it was too late to take them back. There was no stopping the river of tears or the flood of words that kept spilling recklessly from my mouth.

"I don't want to be the Starkeeper! I want to stay with you and

Myriam and Aggie." A huge sob escaped. "I want to marry Glyn!"

I sucked in a breath and squeezed my eyes shut, imagining my life the way I wished it could be with all my might. My skin prickled all over, suspended in this tiny dream of possibility, a perfect vision of Glyn and me happily traveling the Pyxian roads together in our very own wagon ... Glyn and me starting a family, with fat babies bouncing on our laps. Glyn and me—ordinary, happy Pyxies, led down every rutted country road by my loyal, lovable Firefly. Oh, Firefly!

"And I don't want to leave Firefly! *I can't!*" I wailed. "*I won't!*"

Fin's stern voice broke through my daydream, and reality sucked the images away while the painful picture of my destined future came into sharp, ugly focus.

"Jesobel. Don't say that! You can't say that. This is your destiny." He opened my hand and wrapped it around the bottle with his own. "This is what Aggie has worked so hard to train you for. It's the very reason you were born."

I stood stiff as Fin gripped my shoulders and tried to shake some sense into me. His eyes scanned my face in a way that caused shame to burn inside my chest and heat my cheeks. I looked away.

I knew deep inside he was right. Or at least that there was nothing I could do to change my fate. Destiny had given me violet, Mystic eyes. Destiny had killed my mother when I was born on Quickbane afternoon. Destiny had made me the only living descendant of Starkeeper Yarrow. I could have punched destiny in the face if it had one.

"Besides," whispered Fin, his voice grave and barely audible, "you bear the mark, Jesobel. There's no possible way it could be anyone else. It's most certainly you." His eyes were so serious I cringed under their weight. But I had no idea what he meant.

I bore the mark? *What* mark? I felt the phantom needle spin beneath my skin. *No. No, not that. Not that mark...* Something awful clicked inside my head, like puzzle pieces showing a picture I wasn't ready to see. But it was too late.

CHAPTER 6

"Hasn't Aggie t-told you?" Fin stuttered, his face clouded with worry and blotched red with his mistake. I watched his lip twitch, his eyebrows furrow. But he couldn't un-say it, any more than I could un-say how I really felt about becoming our Starkeeper. I pinched my eyebrows at him, a painful lump lodging itself in my throat, an erratic panic dancing behind my ribcage like so many moths too close to a flame.

"I... I just assumed you knew, Jesobel. I mean... I thought you have *always* known..." He looked as confused as I felt, and twice as sorry.

I shook my head in slow motion.

"Really?"

The horrified contortion on my face must have frightened Fin—he tugged me roughly to the shaded side of the tinker's wagon and shoved me against it, lowering his voice to a thin whisper, his hands clutching my shoulders like talons, and squeezed way too hard.

"Listen," he started, an uneasy edge to his voice, his eyes searching for something hidden in mine, "I don't know why Aggie never told you this, but Myriam saw it, the day you were born, Jesobel. The mark. The Compass of Pyxis. *The Heart of Azimuth.*"

I blinked my eyes. I couldn't process what he was saying. I refused to accept it. This couldn't possibly be happening right now. This was a test. One of Aggie's crazy tests... it had to be! Everything I had ever known slipped off-kilter, un-anchored inside of me, untethered itself from all the truths I once clung to. My reality, my whole life, all of my memories changed instantly with this tiny bit of withheld information. How could Aggie keep this from me? How *could* she?

"Listen to me," Fin explained, "the day you were born, the Compass of Pyxis flared bright upon your tiny chest. It lit up the birthing tent like a violet sun before it vanished back into your quickflame. But it was right here." My heart stuttered where he pressed three fingers firmly above it, where it *had* flared up just a few hours ago.

I had subconsciously convinced myself that it was some trick of the amulet. Something Vallax had caused. But it wasn't. I hadn't even thought about it being the Compass of Pyxis, but now... now... I didn't like the way it was starting to make sense in my head.

"It's you, Jessa. You're not *just* the Starkeeper. You are the Heart of Azimuth – the Way-Bringer. *You will lead us back home.*"

My head swam, my hands went clammy and my pulse galloped in my throat. The legend rattled around in my mind, jumbled. Every horrible word of it, bouncing and echoing between my ears as I attempted to make sense of it all.

"It's a legend," I tried to convince myself. "It's only a legend! The Legend of Azimuth is just a stupid, ancient story. A childhood rhyme!"

I gulped air, tried not to cry. I had to find the loophole. It couldn't be true. I couldn't be the one in that terrible prophecy. *No way!*

Fin just looked at me, his blue eyes too serious for words, and squeezed a little tighter.

"Then why hasn't Aggie told me about this, Fin? Why would she keep something this serious from me?" I pushed him away. Panic and anger choked my throat, drying it like an endless dusty road, tightening it so I could scarcely breathe. The flesh where the compass had been itched and burned; I feared it was going to make an appearance again.

Fin just held me with that talon grip, and didn't even blink.

The truth of it began to sink in. Fin was no liar. Fin was the most honest person I had ever known. I could feel that damned compass freezing my skin above my ribcage. The needle twirling at impossible speeds. I was woozy with the memory of it.

"Fin, what does this mean?" I croaked.

But I knew exactly what it meant.

My uncle's voice was tender, reassuring. But he left out the ugly part of what this *really* meant.

His voice was gentle, his grip was not. "It means that you are the one who is going to lead us back to our Lost Realm someday, Jesobel... you carry the way back home to our Lost Realm. Not just the Secret. *The Way*..." Fin's voice trailed off, and I squirmed beneath his claw-like grasp, unsettled by the look in his eyes—a mixture of sadness and dread. He didn't dare say aloud what we were both thinking.

The words, the awful, prophetic words rattled me to the bone as the Legend of Azimuth tumbled wildly in my mind. I didn't want to remember those words. I didn't want them to be true. I wasn't going to be the one to unlock the portal to the Orphic and let unfathomable evil into this world! I couldn't start a war between the Mystic and the Orphic! I couldn't be the one responsible for the possible, probable annihilation of Vale! *I wouldn't!*

I shook my head, unwilling to accept any of it. "No. It's just a legend, Fin. A *legend*," I spat. I tore myself from his grip, panic shifting to a fury that tightened every muscle in my body. My head swam with vertigo. I steadied myself on the wagon behind me. "It can't be true! It can't. Aggie wouldn't keep this from me. She wouldn't just *not* tell me about something this massive, Fin. I will never forgive her. Never!"

"Jessa, shhhh! Don't say that. You know how she is about all her magical stuff and her books and stories and legends. She'll hex you good if she hears you talk like that!"

But there was no possible reason I could fathom that could make this important of an omission acceptable. I couldn't hide the rage that bubbled from nowhere, that felt as if it had brewed there forever, waiting for this exact moment to explode. It had to be a fairy tale. Aggie wouldn't betray me like this. I seethed, unwilling to accept any of it.

"It's only a legend. A stupid centuries-old fairy story. *It has to be, Fin!* Aggie would have prepared me for this!" I turned circles, wringing my hands, rubbing my head, trying to erase all of it from my mind.

"Aggie would have prepared me," I growled again.

But something deep inside of me knew that she *had* been preparing me for this. I was a terrible student. I should have paid more attention... but I didn't ask to be born on Quickbane with stupid Mystic eyes. I didn't even want to be Starkeeper! And now I had to think about *this?* I was the Heart of Azimuth, too? The fate of the world was in *my* sorry hands? My head pounded. I wanted to run.

"Take a breath, Jess." Fin tried to comfort me. "Has Aggie seriously never told you what they saw in that tent? I mean, this is exactly what she has been training you for. I... I honestly don't understand..." His words spilled out in a mumble, almost too quiet for me to hear, but regret tainted every one of them, loud and clear. He was just as baffled as me.

"Yeah, well, nope, she didn't tell me. And nope. I had no idea," I snapped. "I thought I was being trained as a Magic Weaver to prepare for my duty as Starkeeper. To Keep the stupid Secret. Not for *this*. She forgot to mention *THIS!*" My mind spun out of control, my thoughts tumbling from my mouth at atomic speeds as I tried to make sense of it all, to reason it all away. But with each attempt, the compass reminded me of its presence with an icy twinge of pain. Or did it? Did I just imagine that whole thing today? Vallax almost seemed like a hallucination now. I clung briefly to this hope.

"You know what?" said Fin, his voice a little too bright. "Perhaps Myriam *was* just seeing things," he reasoned. "Everyone was exhausted the day you were born. It was so hot. Too hot. The hottest week in history. Maybe she was hallucinating, that's all. Maybe that's why Aggie never told you. Because you're right, Aggie would never keep something this important from you. She wouldn't." He almost sounded convinced. Almost.

"But she did, Fin, didn't she? She *did* keep this from me!" I remembered the way the compass glowed, the wildly spinning needle. My hand flew to my chest and I scratched at the phantom menace, a sensation both dark and powerful pulsing there.

I lunged past Fin, ready to run to the comfort of my horse, but he caught my elbow and spun me back to face him.

"Why didn't she tell me?" I growled. Salty tears licked down my burning cheeks.

For the first time in my life, I missed my mother, or at least the idea of her. I instantly felt unbearably alone, my lip quivering. More tears were about to fall, hard and fast.

My stubborn need to cling to Aggie's loyalty to me was an unraveling thread, in charge of holding the world as I knew it together, organized and true. And that thread was about to break, a frayed disaster. I knew it. I just didn't want to believe it.

"Maybe she was waiting until my birthday to tell me. Or maybe you're right, maybe Myriam *was* seeing things…" I tried to convince myself, but I knew deep down it was a false hope.

"I honestly don't know, Jessa. Look, I'm sorry." Fin's voice was soft, working to comfort me, but it was edged in fear nearly as deep as my own. "I shouldn't have said anything… I'm so sorry."

I was rigid with anger, the more I accepted the story he shared, the deeper the sense of betrayal swirled inside me. The depth of my anger at Aggie frightened me.

Fin pulled me close and hugged me tight. He smelled of wood shavings and paint. Of safety. Of home.

"Please don't tell Aggie I told you about that," he begged. "Whether it's true or not, she'll hex me to the moons and back."

I remained tense beneath his embrace. An icy burn traced around and around the lines, circles and points that made up the compass, dormant, for now, inside my quickflame.

I couldn't tell Uncle Fin that it was true. That I knew for a fact it was true. That the stupid compass had made an appearance just a few hours before. I couldn't tell him because I still didn't want to believe it. He hugged me tighter.

"Please don't tell her," he whispered.

Aggie would be furious with him if she did have other plans to tell me in her own sweet time. Fin didn't deserve her wrath. He honestly thought that she had already told me. I believed that, at least.

And maybe Myriam *had* been hallucinating. Maybe I *was* just overreacting. Maybe it *was* just some weird coincidence, what happened earlier. Maybe it was the fault of that amulet after all.

I drew a deep, cool breath into my lungs and exhaled, letting my anger seep from the soles of my feet into the grass, down, down into the dark Orphic depths of Vale.

"I won't tell her. But you owe me, Finley Black." I melted a little, the wave of fury ebbing some. He let out a huge sigh and smiled a little.

"Your quick temper is going to get you into big trouble someday, Starkeeper Jesobel," he whispered, jamming a finger into my rib and wiggling it.

I fought the tickle with everything I had, but couldn't stop a lopsided smile from creeping across my angry lips. Fin placed a peace-making kiss on top of my head, tucked Starkeeper Yarrow's nyxiegram into my gatherings bag, circled my waist with his arm, and steered me around the wagon and toward the pyre. I took a deep breath. For one second, everything was normal again. Everything was okay.

"You've got some Igniting to do, young lady. And I think a certain *someone* is looking for you." He winked. "What do you say we have some fun!"

I stumbled forward as he shoved me into the throng of merry youth dancing in the dusk around the unlit pyre, every last one of them awaiting my arrival. The Quickfire couldn't be lit without me. Not this year. My stomach was a sick jumble of emotion. I felt detached, somehow, from myself, from the world I knew. And when a whorl of dancers passed, I was a lame animal caught up in a stampede of ruffles and ribbons and music. Everything swirled around me, but it all seemed so far away. I was left standing alone in their wake, my head spinning as fast as their bodies.

My heart raced uneasily when I spotted my green-eyed fiddler at the hub of it all. My gorgeous golden-haired Glyn.

He caught my eye and smiled at me. I ached to be near him, my anchor in this wild sea of confusion. His turquoise bow sawed across the strings, singing a song of freedom.

Freedom, I realized heavily, that would never be mine.

CHAPTER 7

When the Igniting song began, it took all of my strength to focus. I summoned my entire force of illumins with a heavy heart, and felt the ticklish buzz as they threaded from the mystic portal near my sternum to dance around the pyre, gathering in number as all of the children's spark fairies joined them, one by one.

People gasped when my fairies kept coming and coming. It was the first time I'd summoned them all in front of anyone but Aggie, and they came in staggering numbers. The only person smiling was Zuzu Sparx, who would summon her immense force of illumins on Quickbane for the fairyworks show. Her droves of tiny mystic beings made my vast army seem miniscule.

The countless tiny, winged creatures glowed and bobbed around the unlit Quickfire logs, circling thirteen times, once for each moon tree, as we sang the ethereal Igniting song. The soft words came out of my mouth, but for the first time in my life, I felt totally disconnected from them. And from my fairies. From Glyn. From Aggie. From everything.

I writhed inside my own skin, acutely aware of the haughty glances that flew like daggers from the other girls. Clearly, they were all glad to see me go, and were finally unafraid to show it during these last days when I could barely still be counted as one of them. As ordinary. As family. In a few days, I'd be gone. At last, they would have their chance at wooing Glyn.

I tried to lift my chin and act like I belonged in the royal shoes I would soon fill, but the fury I'd felt earlier returned when Seraphina sidled up to Glyn and stole a smile from him. It was a small gesture, but it burned and I couldn't pull myself together.

The furtive looks from the adults told me that I wasn't the only person who felt I wasn't cut out to be Starkeeper. Nobody took me seriously, and cold doubt colored their unkind glances. I ached to look to Glyn for some small comfort, but kept my eyes on the pyre as Aggie had taught me. The spark fairies swirled and danced, their lights casting colors and shadows across the faces of young and old alike until the song finally calmed to a melodic hum and then to nothing at all.

This silence was my cue to begin.

I closed my eyes, anger seething in the fast-moving molecules of my quickflame. I tried to calm myself, and whispered the lighting charm with all of the Pyxie children. I took the wreath of quickbane from atop my head and placed it on the pyre. I felt the Mystic quickflame surge through me, connect with the ground at my feet and zoom to the waiting moon tree logs with a ferocity that nearly knocked me backward.

"Ow!" The two boys on either side of me dropped my hands, blowing on their scalded fingers as the quickbane wreath and then the pyre burst into impossibly tall flames with a sizzling hiss and a series of deafening cracks. Massive amethyst flames exploded ever upward, licking far too high into the night, crackling angrily with a spectacular shower of fiery purple sparks. My quickflame dwarfed the entire scene with its mighty presence, casting long, flickering shadows all the way to the north wall. I was mortified. This was the worst time yet.

Why did my magic always seem to have a mind of its own?

Because you're a terrible student, Jesobel. Aggie's scolding words echoed through the empty caverns of my heart.

The Quickfire continued to rip up into the night, clawing its way toward the clouds, popping and hissing. The children closest to the pyre screamed and ran. The circle scattered without ceremony as everyone fled in horror, dodging tiny, fiery violet comets while flashing nasty glares my way. I wanted to vanish. But I couldn't get my legs to work.

I stood frozen, humiliated by the unruly explosive power of my magic, recalling the multitude of times it had betrayed me in front of my peers, gaining me a wide berth and funny looks for the past five years. I always had Glyn to take the edge off those looks. But now? I didn't even see him in all of the confusion.

I felt the burn of Aggie's disapproving gaze searing me from somewhere near, but I couldn't bear to look. I knew by the gasps and murmurs that everyone was staring at me, and I wanted to flee, but my feet wouldn't move, and all I could do was watch my obnoxiously massive violet quickflame lick skyward like dragon's breath, and wish to become invisible.

When I thought I might shrivel and die of absolute humiliation, Glyn came to the rescue with his fiddle, and relief spread over me like a soothing embrace, which, thankfully, shrank the intensity of the flames a little.

"May the Quickfire burn bright for five prosperous nights! Let's dance in honor of our Royal Starkeeper-in-Waiting, Lady Jesobel Vine!" Glyn's hoots and hollers infected the crowd and soon, my humiliating purple flames died down, along with most of the disapproving looks.

Music, laughter and singing rang out once again, while pretty maidens flashed colorful ribbons and petticoats as they twirled around the Quickfire, rosy-cheeked and flirtatious, sweeping nervous boys into the whirlpool as they passed, a rainbow of spark fairies dancing above their heads, bells tinkling at their ankles. Visions of absolute loveliness.

I breathed a sigh of relief, edging out of the tornado of silk and giggling maidens and looked for Glyn, who was swallowed into the crowd with his fiddle humming a boisterous tune.

He circled around, and then stopped, stamping his foot in the dirt to keep time as he played. As I watched Glyn, he smiled at the world with such comforting warmth that the knot of tense emotions in my chest, the sharp hum of my quickflame, calmed and finally made way for sweet, ticklish butterflies to settle in my stomach, along with the tingling memory of his kiss.

I moved toward him with purpose, with gladness, with a fierce desire to be wrapped in his arms, to feel the relief of being close to him, and to tell him everything Fin had said, to tell him about my secret—the compass hiding under my flesh. And more than anything, I wanted to kiss him again. This time, madly, deeply, with all of my heart.

With this sudden wave of emotion filling my heart to overflowing, I realized, finally, that I had to find a way to marry Glyn, stupid tradition or not. He always said he would do anything to make it work, even if I was going to be gone most of the moons each year. I didn't want to live without Glyn. I couldn't imagine my life without him. He always said he would be the one to break that dumb old tradition which hinted that Pyxie Starkeepers weren't made for love.

I had almost fought my way to him when Seraphina swooped past, nearly knocking me over to deftly whisper in Glyn's ear and plant a kiss on his lips mid-twirl. Glyn's sea-green eyes twinkled merrily as they met hers, a secret smile erupting between them.

My stomach curdled and sank to my feet. My knees wobbled. My head spun. Everything became dark and ugly so fast.

Had Glyn finally listened to me? The millions of times when I told him it would be unfair of me to marry him, that I couldn't bear the guilt of leaving him alone most of the year? That traditions existed for reasons, even if those reasons seemed stupid? That Aggie had warned me a thousand times that if I truly loved him, I would let Glyn go? What had I done?

When Seraphina flitted away, I stood rooted to the ground, unable to process what I had just seen. And though his fingers flew and his bow sawed across the strings and the girls and boys kept circling the Quickfire, time came to a halt for one horrific moment, and I failed to hide the devastation painted across my face.

And that's when Glyn finally saw me.

By the time he blinked his guilty green eyes, I was gone, a mass of whispering spark fairies gossiping after me.

CHAPTER 8

I stumbled back to our shoppe, leaving my people and my horrible igniting fiasco behind, queasy with heartache. Firefly nickered and crept out of the shadows, nuzzling me where I stood staring into the coals of Aggie's cookfire, sick with the image of that giggling blue-eyed redhead swooping in to plant that kiss on Glyn's lips. It played over and over in my mind and I couldn't make it stop.

I parked my small forehead against my horse's massive warm cheek, stroked his fuzzy ear and imagined myself shooting a satisfying number of arrows at that dumb girl.

Firefly's huge jaw muscles moved beneath my forehead as he chewed a fragrant mouthful of tender spring grass. This simple, comforting motion, and the sweet alfalfa scent of his breath, the bright musk of his coat, was all it took for the tears to start flowing. I buried my face into his mane and cried.

I listened to him chew as my heartbeat rose between my ears, thumping there until I was deaf to anything but my increasing sobs, the shackles of my predetermined destiny tightening, crushing my spirit. My spark fairies hovered around us, playing in Firefly's long mane and looking a bit anxious to return to their home in the Mystic.

Firefly gave no answer, but listened intently as he yanked another hank of grass from the ground and savored it.

"Go on, Liliet," I said to the only fairy who had yet shared her name with me. She linked her tiny hands with the others and I felt the ticklish buzz in my ribcage of them returning to the Mystic in a long chain, one by one.

"You chew like a cow, Firefly." I needed a distraction or my head would explode. "Look here," I said, between jerky, heaving breaths. I pulled a stack of folded parchment scraps from the leather gatherings bag belted at my hip and shook it at my stallion.

"I am having an impossible time drawing you. See?" I said, shuffling through the scribbles. I dug into my pocket for the most recent attempt and showed it to him. "You look like a spotted sausage with legs. Who will want their family, their people, Guarded by a Pyxie with a four-legged sausage gilded above her wagon door? I can't do this! I don't want to!" I kicked the bantam cage. The hens squawked, feathers twirling about.

"Do you know what Fin told me tonight? He said that I bear the mark. That *I* am the Heart of Azimuth. The Way-Bringer. That the compass from this afternoon is the very compass from the legend. It can't be true! Can it?"

My horse nickered. My heart sank.

"This isn't good, is it? It means that really, really, realllllly bad things are going to happen! And they will be all my fault!" I gave a last big sob, comforted only slightly by how ridiculous what I had just told my horse sounded aloud. The Heart of Azimuth? The Way-Bringer? Me? No. It couldn't *possibly* be true! My stomach churned.

But it was true, wasn't it? I considered kicking the bantam cage again, but then felt sorry for the little hens who were just settling down from my last attack. Instead, I shredded my most recent drawing into a million tiny pieces and ignited them, only I tried a little harder to control the intensity of the flames this time. But of course, I failed.

Firefly ignored the explosion and the hissing shower of violet sparks, and calmly ripped up another juicy knot of grass near my foot, sooty remnants of paper curling near his hooves. I sighed, kissed his furry cheek, and turned for bed, exhausted from crying and stupid secrets and legends compasses and annoying redheads.

With a heavy heart, I finally acknowledged the truth. In four days, everything would change. I couldn't have Glyn. Especially if I really was the Heart of Azimuth. I was about to embark on a lone journey to Corona Australis to become the Royal Starkeeper of my people. To live a life of service. A life I never asked for. A life I didn't want. A life that nobody believed I was qualified for. And they were right.

And even worse, the entire fate of Vale might lie in my sorely incapable hands. I felt like I might vomit.

CHAPTER 9

"Oh, Firefly." I collapsed into the strength of his soft neck, seeking comfort, but the heavy pull of all of it—of stupid Seraphina and Glyn... the icy burn of the compass ... Aggie's betrayal for keeping it a secret... the nyxiegram I still hadn't read. I stroked his ear and kissed his cheek, kicked dirt onto the dying flames and slowly made my way to the wagon, sleep my only prospect for comfort of any sort. I was intercepted by a skinny boy with hay in his unkempt hair, who appeared like a ghost from the shadows. He stank faintly of sour horse piss and hay.

"Might I?" he said, reaching out to touch Firefly's mane. His accent was from Rockwall—clearly not brightborn, but that of some lowly dunborn middling by the thick of it. Still, even the lowliest servant commanded more respect in Rockwall than any Pyxian did. Even a soon-to-be Royal Starkeeper.

Despite my foul mood, I attempted to be kind and welcomed the distraction from my tangled thoughts. "Of course." I forced a smile, letting Firefly mouth my palm with his fat lips, looking for a nonexistent treat.

I was proud of my stallion. Fin gave him to me when I turned three, which was also Firefly's third birthday. By the time he was strong enough to hold riders, I was comfortable bareback in no time flat. For years we rode alongside the caravan, zipping between Fin's wagon, Aggie's wagon and Glyn's wagon, until Aggie put me and Firefly in charge of driving when her old dapple mare finally returned to the Mystic.

"He's pretty friendly," I said.

"Certainly, milady. That 'e is," said the boy. "Quite friendly, indeed." He stroked Firefly's massive cheek and scratched behind his lucky white ear.

"Such unusual markin's!" The boy marveled, looking impressed as he regarded Firefly's striking colors.

Firefly snorted and pawed at the earth, tossing his head so his ridiculously long mane flew around in impressive waves.

"He's a special one, ain't 'e," said the stranger. "Ain't never seen the likes. Them colors... remarkable. A real stunner!"

"He's the only horse we've ever bred that turned up with his coloring. Pretty, isn't he?"

"It's as if someone went an' tossed a bucket o' starry night sky on 'im! Why, you could see an 'orse like that comin' from a league away!"

The boy stood back and regarded Firefly like only an experienced horseman would do, with a glint of true admiration in his eye.

"Fit fer royalty, that 'orse," he said. "Fit fer royalty," he repeated, mainly to himself.

"He can definitely be a royal pain in the arse, if that's what you mean." I laughed. Firefly snorted and stomped a hoof in protest.

"Do you ride?" I asked.

The boy nodded, lost in thought, scratching Firefly's sweet spot behind his jaw that makes him drool a little.

I whispered to Firefly, and a secret answer passed between us, too subtle for the boy to notice.

"Would you like to take him for a trot down the lane?"

"Oh, wouldn't I, milady!" His face lit up like he'd just seen up a girl's skirt for the first time. "Truly, wouldn't I ever!" The boy stroked Firefly's nose and got a soft nicker out of him.

"He likes you. He's picky, you know. You should consider yourself lucky. He doesn't let just anyone ride. Here, hop on." I held out my clasped hands to give him a leg up.

The boy settled easily on Firefly's back, like he'd ridden him a million times before, which was a bit confusing. Firefly was usually stubborn with any other riders but me, even riders who got his rare stamp of approval, Aggie being the only exception to his stubbornness.

With a gigantic grin, the boy navigated my horse effortlessly around the graying cookfire coals, whispering to Firefly with little more than his body language. I guessed that he must be the Starkeeper's stable boy, his rapport with Firefly so unlike anything I'd ever seen.

I followed them to our lane, and watched as the boy cycled Firefly through several gaits, surprised that he dared gallop without bridle or saddle. Middlings were notoriously addicted to their leathery vices and thought us Pyxies savages for riding so raw and so free without any tack to speak of. But he rode like the wind, and didn't seem ill at ease in the least.

For several laps up and down the lane, I stood in awe of how beautiful and regal my horse looked being ridden by someone whose skill matched my own. I had never really had a chance to notice how remarkably he moved, arching his neck like a taught rainbow, tucking his feet so high when he trotted. The boy even had him backing up, walking sideways and turning circles as if he'd been training with him for years.

When the pair returned, the boy's cheeks were ruddy with cool air. Firefly blew a gust from his nostrils. It was clear they had bonded.

"You're quite the horseman!" I said, both impressed and slightly annoyed.

"I just 'ave an affinity is all. Comes from years of workin' in

Rowan's stables I s'pose. I respect 'em. The animals. We understand one another." He slid off Firefly and gave him a pat on the flank. "Don't we, boy?" He smiled shyly and stood back to admire my steed one last time.

"B'sides, that's quite an animal yeh've got there, fit fer royalty. Fit fer royalty n'deed." He smiled warmly at me, and I realized that this filthy dunborn boy had cheered me from my sour mood. I leaned over and gave him a peck on the cheek.

"You can come back and visit us again if you like," I said, grinning. "You don't know how much you've cheered me."

The boy's cheeks went pink, and he shyly stuck a hand in his pocket to fiddle with some tinkling coins, when something like a sudden idea passed across his brow. He chuckled, gave a shy, grateful nod and Firefly a final pat, and disappeared into the night.

"Hey, what's your name?" I called after him. But the boy was already gone.

I dismissed him with a playful shrug and kissed Firefly goodnight. "That boy could ride, Firefly. What did you think?" Firefly snorted and lowered his head and nickered low. "Shoshono fheelo, Firefly," I whispered. "You are my favorite fuzzy friend." He nuzzled his nose into my palm, and I was sorry I didn't have an apple for him.

Weary beyond reason, but feeling slightly less horrid, I climbed into my berth below Aggie's at the back of the wagon, pulled the sliding doors closed until not a crack of light greeted my eye, and summoned Liliet and her closest kin so I could draw until Aggie returned from the Quickfire... and to listen for the knock below my berth that would mean Glyn hadn't completely forgotten that I existed.

With a book as a desk, propped up on my mother's somewhat tattered, yet beautiful Andromedan pillows—the jasmine sachets inside still faintly aromatic after sixteen years—I scribbled and erased until nearly dawn to the light of Liliet's family. I had been curious about her itty bitty swelling belly, eager to meet her baby. I loved to watch her wild, wispy hair move about her head as if she were always battling a private little windstorm. It had an almost electric life of its own. My illumins delighted in making silly faces at me, and entertaining me with acrobatics. I loved them with all of my heart.

With my drawing nearly finished, my mind slipped back to Glyn, and then immediately shifted to nasty thoughts about that nasty redheaded girl. I barely slept.

Hours after I heard the wooden squeaks and groans of Aggie climbing into her berth, and with the old woman's soft snoring filling the wagon, I lay awake waiting, and hoping. And then wondering with a heavy heart why Glyn hadn't come to see me. He always knocked below my berth on the first night of the Quickfire. Perhaps he was knocking on Seraphina's berth now. My stomach slipped sideways. I fought back another wave of tears.

He could have at least waited until I was gone to take up with that frilly ginger pinwheel!

Even though I knew in my heart that it was a stupid idea, I pushed thoughts of that awful Seraphina aside, and clung to the hope of hearing that knock.

CHAPTER 10

I awoke from a brief and fitful sleep to Aggie's loud, irritated voice as she scraped the berth doors open without even attempting to be quiet. My heart sank. Glyn never came.

Unbearably bright light flooded in to torment my eyes. I growled and rolled to face the other way, pulling a pillow over my head, feeling cross and needing more rest. Hours more.

Lingering bits and pieces of a dream tugged at the outskirts of my consciousness. A dark wolf and a white wolf, snarling and tearing each other's throats out. A bright needle on a ghostly compass spinning crazily. A light-haired woman with sad, bright eyes, holding a star cupped in her hands. A mysterious malevolent whisper tugging at my quickflame: *Find it… Release me…*

Aggie's terse voice cut through the dream-haze. "Up you go, Jessa! It's Flaxday. The next three days are crucial. It's time for you to learn the first hex in the Venoms Trivium."

Aggie used her ultra-serious voice, the one without even a hint of playfulness to it. I tensed, feeling wound too tight, and I hadn't even opened my eyes yet. It was going to be a long day.

I rubbed my eyelids and crawled out of the berth, disappointed by my drawing now that I saw it in the morning light.

Hideous. Again.

I only had three days left to get it right. Ugh. I crumpled it up and chucked it in the wood stove, satisfied to watch it curl at the edges and burst into a hot orange flame before disintegrating into nothingness. Without having to use any spastic magic at all! Ah, to be normal…

"Come on, eat, eat. I can't believe you slept in this morning, Jessa!" The bite in Aggie's voice stung. She had been this way for months. I thought for sure she'd have been a little softer, a little kinder, the closer we got to the big day. Guess I was wrong.

"I'm sorry, Aggie. I was up half the night trying to draw Firefly again. I failed miserably." I pouted, smoothing out my skirts, a wrinkled mess from sleeping in them. I tried to tame my wild hair using my fingers as a comb, without success, and considered telling Aggie about Vallax, the amulet, and the compass. I was so angry at her for not mentioning the compass, I didn't know how to bring it up. *Better to just say it*, I decided.

I opened my mouth to speak, but shrank in silence as she cut disapproving eyes at me.

The painted wagon door stood open and beyond the bright rectangle of light, smoke from the morning's cookfire drifted inside. A plate of honeycakes, as cold as Aggie's glare, sat on the fold-down table just inside the door with a mug of equally chilly tea.

The dance Aggie and I did to navigate the small space inside the wagon was something we didn't even think about, it just came naturally. Not once had either of us bumped the other in the head with a cupboard door, or found ourselves face to face unsure of which way to step to let the other pass. We could be blindfolded and we'd still know how to get around each other without a hitch.

But my days of dancing with Aggie were numbered. I slogged toward my breakfast with a melancholy heart and a needling ache to speak with Glyn. To feel his arms around me one last time. An ache that was beginning to fester like some sort of poisonous thorn wound. Beneath that ache was the betrayal I felt about the whole Legend of Azimuth thing—did Aggie plan to tell me about that anytime soon? And that weird dream... that creepy voice. Gave me the chills. I scratched my chest where the compass had been, an imaginary itch crawling there.

Why hasn't she said anything about it yet? I felt so mad at Aggie, but I couldn't do anything about it. If I didn't focus today, it would be the end of me. I swallowed down my anger and tried to focus on the day ahead.

Aggie flipped open a cupboard and began pulling down vials and herbs for the Venoms Trivium—the only truly dark magic I would ever be allowed to learn. The racket made my head pound, and I felt certain that Aggie was clanking her glass jars together on purpose. I sighed, not in the mood to spend my day with a cranky Magic Weaver, and tried to choke down the honeycakes and cold tea, but my appetite vanished.

"Did you visit Franci this morning?" I asked, poking at the cakes. I needed to get Aggie's mind off my bad sleeping habits so she would quit banging things around, and so I could stop feeling so guilty for sleeping in. And so my head would stop aching. And so we could just get this day over with. So I could finally go and find Glyn. And say goodbye to him. Or win him back. Or say goodbye... ugh!

"I did," said Aggie curtly. She wasn't ready to forgive me just yet.

"So, how is she? How are the triplets?" I asked, trying to lighten the mood.

"They are just fine, Jesobel. Now eat your food, we need to go into Dryden Forest outside the wall today. We don't need any small talk cluttering up your mind. Shush. Think of your studies."

I sulked and tried to enjoy my cold honeycakes, but felt too wretched, and just a little bit too annoyed to really savor them. I choked down a few bites and washed them down with a mouthful of cold tea, my appetite completely ruined.

Aggie packed her things into a bag and I watched her. I noticed suddenly how old she looked. When had her face become a dried apricot, etched with deep ravines everywhere? There was a toughness about her, despite her birdlike limbs, so thin and lithe, and I noticed with no small shock that her signature blouse—pale sage embroidered cotton with billowy three-quarter length sleeves—sagged sadly on her aged arms. Aggie's twinkly blue eyes were somewhat wide set, framing a nose that was once dainty and lovely, but that time had deemed—practically overnight—no more than a necessary appendage, rather than an alluring feature.

As she filled a leather satchel with cups, a bottle of cider, and two sandwiches that smelled delicious, I noticed a weighty tiredness settle on her brow that I'd never seen before. The sight of her looking so frail unnerved me.

"Aggie… are you okay?" I asked, regretting it immediately.

"Of course," she snapped. "I'm fine! Now hurry up and wash your dishes. Where are your boots? There's no time to lose."

Flustered, I did as I was told and found my boots outside under the stairs. I begrudgingly shoved my toes in one by one without any socks and laced them up, not looking forward to learning dark magic from such a grouchy woman, or to wearing sweaty boots on such a beautiful spring day. A day which should be enjoyed barefoot and frolicking. *With Glyn,* I caught myself thinking. I needed to stop being so wishy-washy about him! *Besides, Seraphina has his heart now,* I reminded myself with disgust.

I whistled for Firefly and he waltzed around the corner. I put a pad on his back for Aggie's bony bum, and a delicately braided bitless bridle with matching reins and beaded tassels—a gift from a seafaring Pyxie who was taken by Firefly's beauty at the Hazel Moon Faire, and insisted I have it. Aggie would never admit it, but she loved that fancy bridle. Firefly tolerated it, only for her.

"Firefly is ready for you! I'm going to go get Pennyfeathers," I shouted, leaning my head into the wagon. "I'll be right back!" Aggie didn't answer. "Aggie! I'll be right back," I shouted louder, for good measure. She was getting so deaf. Then I turned and jogged into the lane, cutting across rows of shoppes, scanning swaying shoppe signs for *Fin's Custom Wagons* to borrow Myriam's mare.

By the time I returned to our wagon with Penny, Aggie was astride Firefly looking fierce and impatient. She trotted off when she saw us, forcing us to catch up.

"Today you will learn the Viperberry Hex. On Sorrelday, the Bleakhound Hex. At midnight on the eve of Quickbane, you will learn the Ghostmoth Hex. We have no time to waste, Jesobel. I expect you to pay close attention. The Venoms Trivium are incredibly dangerous." She shot me a look that made me feel small. She did that a lot.

I felt a bit dark and heavy inside, and somewhat agitated, and in no mood for hexes. I clucked Pennyfeathers into a trot to keep up with Aggie and Firefly.

As we headed toward the northwest gate, we passed Glyn. My heart fluttered. I slowed Penny to a walk. I wanted to stop, to embrace him and tell him we'd find a way to marry, just like he always said we would. That I loved him more than anything else in the world, and that nothing would make me happier than being his wife, even if that meant hardly seeing each other at all. *Even if that means dragging him into the Legend of Azimuth*, I admitted, pushing the guilt of such a selfish thought aside.

Then I remembered the kiss he got from Seraphina, and a hot stab of jealousy impaled my heart. I pretended not to see him. He jogged toward me with a big grin on his face, but I kept my eyes forward and shifted Penny into a canter until I was riding alongside Aggie, a furious heat flashing in my belly. From anger or guilt, I wasn't sure anymore.

As I passed Glyn, seeing him only from the corner of my eye, I saw his smile fall away, leaving a hurt, confused expression on his face.

Serves him right. Stupid redhead.

But as we drew farther away, the stabby feeling in my heart changed into heavy regret. I wanted to turn back! I wanted to apologize.

"Aggie, may I please just stop for one sec–" I asked as politely as possible, looking guiltily back at Glyn's stupefied face.

"No," she cut me off. And that was that.

CHAPTER 11

ggie's mood didn't improve even after we trotted through the gate and deep into the forest. She quizzed me on every plant we passed, forcing me to remember a zillion things about each one: How to call on their assistance, even from afar. How to summon their energies and weave them into a powerful charm, enchantment or spell. What this petal or that stamen could heal, unlock, repair, befuddle, confound, freeze, conceal or stop, and so on. Why this one was safe and that one was dangerous, whether that one will naturally summon Orphic magic or Mystic magic, and how to handle this deadly plant with Orphic roots, and that one with paralyzing Orphic seedpods. It was the same for every bird, vole and squirrel that flitted away in our wake.

She quizzed me on the seven elements and their uses, and dozens of creatures with an abundance of Mystic magic, most of which I had never even seen in my life and probably never would, but she assured me their magic could be summoned regardless. She made me recite the difference between quickflame and devilsflare—the Mystic and Orphic energy of all living things, where all magic exists. She reminded me that I would need to spend the next year abroad mastering my ability to harness magic when Starkeeper Yarrow would take me under her wing during the long journey aboard the Queen's silver ship to Corona

Australis. I was to finish my training until I could control my quickflame, and safely weave any type of magic, Mystic or Orphic, without even thinking about it. And without lighting anything on fire or causing mysterious rashes to erupt on anyone's skin within a two-league radius.

"And maybe you'll put a little more effort into your studies with the good Starkeeper than you have with me," Aggie snapped.

I was as focused as possible, but I couldn't help it that Glyn was heavy on my mind. I was feeling really bad for ditching him without stopping to say hello. Or goodbye. Whatever. For months I'd been telling him to back off, why did I suddenly want him all to myself? Why would I even entertain the idea that we could somehow make it work out between us? *Pyxie Starkeepers don't marry for a reason, Jesobel. You better think long and hard about what's best for that boy.* Aggie's raspy voice of reason echoed through my cavernous heart, a mantra I'd been repeating to myself—and to Glyn—for two years.

By the time we reached a small clearing after an hour's ride, my brain was so frazzled that all I could think about was that sandwich Aggie had packed. And a nap. And I wanted to know why Aggie was constantly looking over her shoulder as if we were being followed. We weren't— she had gone out of her way to weave a windowroot charm as soon as we reached the edge of the woods. She tied the supple roots into a little circle and braided it into her hair with a silver thread, activating it with a string of words that conjured a swirling Mystic window inside the circle, which would keep tabs on anyone nearby.

I'd seen her use the charm once before. One time, a man within the charm's radius appeared inside the window, and she went all weird until she saw through his eyes and basically embodied him until she had enough information to know if he had meant us any harm. It was creepy, I can say that much.

The whole idea of this entire day was making me wish more than ever that I could go back to the marketplace and find Glyn and just run away with him to live a regular, boring, un-magical Pyxie life. All of this Magic Weaver and Starkeeper business made me weary and anxious. And never mind that stupid compass, and what *that* meant.

I could get used to the way my hand felt folded up in Glyn's, the way his strong arms held me close. The clove and licorice scent of soap that clung to his skin. I could get used to kissing him every day, I realized, with another flash of jealousy. That stupid Seraphina certainly seemed very cozy planting her lips on his. My already sour mood festered into something seriously ugly.

There was an awkward silence, during which my stomach growled loudly while Aggie set up a few magical items on a huge, smooth tree stump.

"I need to know that you're ready, Jesobel, that you're *capable*," declared Aggie, with an exasperated sigh. I didn't know what to say. I didn't know if I was ready. Or capable. In fact, I was fairly confident that I was neither of those things.

She placed some items in a circle on the stump. A small blue, liquid-filled vial topped with a cork. Seven hard, black berries, or maybe pebbles, which plinked crazily around in a clear corked jar like legless, faceless fleas caught in a tiny tornado. And something that looked like the bloody, hooked fang of some slithering, venomous reptile. I knew better than to ask questions before we began, so instead I asked if we could have lunch, by announcing that I was starving. I tried not to whine when I said it.

"There's no need to yell, Jesobel. I can hear you just fine," she cautioned, scrunching her eyebrows at me and looking around suspiciously.

"I'm sorry, Aggie," I said, but I was puzzled. Because she was practically deaf and the only way she ever heard a word I said was if I yelled. And there was that windowroot charm protecting us from prying eyes. Why was she acting so paranoid?

"Can we just eat lunch before we start? Please?" I couldn't help it. I whined.

"Fine." Aggie grabbed my wrist and squeezed with her bony fingers. "But I want you to pay close attention today. The Venoms Trivium come from dark Orphic magic. The darkest. And if you don't master your control over Orphic and Mystic magic, terrible things can happen. Deadly, awful things. These three hexes are for emergencies only, understand? These aren't like Mystic hexes, Jesobel." She held a sandwich up, but wouldn't hand it over until I'd agreed.

"I understand, Aggie," I answered in a whisper, feeling like a scolded child.

"Do you?" she asked again, withholding my lunch and squeezing harder. I lowered my eyes to the ground.

"Yes, Aggie." Just when I thought she couldn't possibly believe in me any less.

She finally let go of my wrist and relinquished the cloth-wrapped bundle. My mouth watered when I caught a whiff of the cheesy goodness inside, but I felt ashamed somehow and nearly lost my appetite again.

"Good girl. I know I can count on you, Jesobel. You were born to do this, you know. It's your destiny to be the Starkeeper of our people."

"I know," I agreed quietly. Reluctantly.

"In more ways than one," she said, somewhat ominously.

The words made my chest itch and I became suspicious about the legend, and had a fleeting sense that this is what she was secretly talking about. I wanted to ask, but I almost didn't want to find out that it was, without doubt, true. Even though I knew it was, I didn't want to learn for sure that she had been keeping this from me my whole entire life. And I didn't want her to get mad at me.

Instead, I repeated what I'd heard a million times, "I know. It's an honor and a privilege..."

Blah blah blah, I said inside my head, ripping into the soft bread and guiltily savoring the herbed cheese and tomatoes inside.

But what if I didn't *want* this honor? My appetite vanished.

We sat down on a log and dug into our food, mine tasting like sawdust despite the flavorful cheese. Aggie was silent. I took a bite and chewed slowly, remembering the kiss Glyn and I shared under the dappled sunlight in the apple grove. Try as I might to focus on the hex, I could not get him out of my mind.

A deep, foreign voice sent a zip of tingles from the base of my spine to the hollow at the back of my skull and frightened me stiff, ejecting me from my dreamy memory. I looked at Aggie. The voice came from her lips, but was not her own:

"I've just had the most brilliant idea!" Every hair on my body stood on end. The windowroot charm! It was working... I looked inside the circular windowroot braided into Aggie's hair, and was shocked to see Ethan Rowan's face!

"We need to banish magic. It was magic that killed our parents, Brother. Filthy Pyxie magic! They must be stopped!" Ethan's windowed likeness looked manic and agitated. The image then shifted and showed the next speaker, Ethan's twin, Evan.

"You're wrong, Ethan. You are paranoid, Brother. It's an effect of all the gambling you do. If you would have stayed at home and trained for our duty instead of sailing off to Ophiucus for women and wine and high-stakes desert horse races, you wouldn't behave this way. Our realm is at stake, that's true. But it's not magic that threatens our stability. It's our Starkeeper, Ethan. It's you." Evan looked disgusted and frustrated.

"You're just bitter that I'm in charge now. Because I was born first. By thirty whole seconds! Ha ha! Besides, you haven't been where I've been. I've sailed around the world. You've stayed here living the old ways, in the dark ages, when the rest of the world progresses. You don't know what they say of our secluded, antiquated realm. We are

the laughing stock of the entire planet. A global joke! We are known as the Pyxie Friends across Vale. They think we pander to the Pyxies with our Quickbane Festival. Those thieving, lying, filthy, magic-wielding witches! You have no idea what the world is like outside this pathetic realm, or what such an opinion could do to harm it. I am going to banish magic in our realm. And any Pyxie caught using magic will be imprisoned. Indefinitely." The venom in Ethan's voice made my blood run cold.

"You can't just banish magic. That's like banishing air! Did you learn nothing in your studies? Besides, Pyxies are harmless folk. I don't believe for one moment that Helix Airheart paid a Magic Weaver to hex the sword that killed our parents. There has to be another explanation."

"Ah, but there isn't. Why else would Helix be in hiding, running from the realm he's next in line to govern? He wanted revenge for his mother and his herd's deaths!"

"I just don't see it, Ethan. The Airhearts are not murderers. If Helix had a vengeful bone in his body, he would have sought revenge for the death of his father years ago. Axis was killed by that Hydran Starkeeper's temperamental nephew. Remember that? So scandalous, everyone in the Eighty-Eight Realms wanted to see that kid put to death! Nobody more than Helix. He worshipped his father. And yet, Helix let the authorities handle it. He's not a murderer, Ethan. Besides, I've seen what you've been doing, Brother. I've seen you dabbling with that book you found. The grimoire that summons Orphic magic! How can you banish magic when you yourself are recklessly wielding it?"

I shuddered, hugging myself. So creepy. Aggie was as still as the log she sat on as she spoke in voices not her own. I chewed slowly and stared, horrified and fascinated all at once. I wanted to shake her and snap her out of it, but I knew it was useless. She would come out when she was ready. I cast my eyes around the forest, and listened again, but neither hoof beats nor footsteps drew near and the only racket came from a skittish squirrel rustling in the leaves.

"You don't know what you're talking about, dear Evan. You have no idea. Why would I play with magic? You're ridiculous. Magic killed our parents! You are delusional, Brother." Ethan's voice sounded like that of someone who had been caught in a lie. The very idea that he might be messing around with Orphic magic was chilling.

"I hope you are telling the truth, for your own sake. This realm needs a good Starkeeper, not an imperious, egotistical, reckless brat who dabbles in dark magic and banishes good magic!"

"Trust me," Ethan's syrupy voice lied. *"You have nothing to worry about. I know what I'm doing, and my reign will take its place in the history of Vale as absolutely unforgettable."*

"Oh, I don't doubt that," spat a sarcastic Evan. *"I don't doubt that one bit."*

Aggie's eyes had gone utterly white and she sat perfectly still. Her ghostly eyelids fluttered, and there was a grave look in her pale blue eyes when they returned from the charm. My heart hammered in my chest and the creepy feeling that made my hair stand on end bloomed into an encompassing fear that caused my eyes to well up.

"Where are they? How close are they?" I whispered to Aggie, shivering in my boots, despite the warmth of the sun.

"They are in Rowan Tower, Jesobel. We are safe," Aggie said, touching my arm in a comforting way, "for now." A dark shadow passed across her face, and I knew there was something she wasn't telling me.

"What was all that? Why did your charm reach that far?" I felt uneasy about all of this, it didn't make sense. Anger boiled somewhere deep inside at the cruel words Ethan said about my people, about magic being banished. And about Pyxies being imprisoned.

"Jesobel, we need to hurry. You need to learn the Venoms Trivium before that pompous Starkeeper starts poking his nose where it doesn't belong. You heard what he said. If we are caught, it means imprisonment.

But I simply can't send you to the Queen's ship without the Venoms Trivium. And if Evan is right... if Ethan is dabbling in Orphic magic..." Her voice trailed off and her face screwed up into a tight, distressed prune. "We better get to work," she mumbled.

"Okay," I agreed. There was an uncomfortable flutter way down in my belly, and a heaviness that clouded my mind. I hoped I could concentrate, but I was distracted by the questions rushing through my own thoughts.

How could Ethan Rowan banish magic in an entire realm? What if he really was dabbling with dark magic? Would he send people out to look for Magic Weavers to arrest them? It was true that all Pyxies have a connection to the Mystic. We are all born with the ability to summon our spark fairies and weave a few simple spells without any real training, but there are very few who are actually trained Magic Weavers and have full access to the power of the Mystic and the Orphic. The smallest handful. Would Aggie be safe once I'd begun my journey to Corona Australis? My stomach refused any more of the sandwich; an unease settled in next to it deep in my gut.

Aggie took a breath and picked up the jar with the bouncing pebbles inside. They clicked frantically on the glass and thudded against the wide cork stopper.

"Viperberry beetles," said Aggie, holding the jar out for me to inspect. "From Lacerta." I peered in at them. They were dark silvery black, the color of hematite, and perfectly round, about the size of floatberries. I could barely make out tiny red eyes. They jetted to and fro on invisible legs, springing upward like fleas, but bashing their tiny bodies against the glass didn't seem to tire them or stop them from behaving so stupidly.

"What are they for?" I asked, knowing Aggie's elusive answer before I had a chance to take back my dumb question.

"The Viperberry Hex, Jesobel," she snipped. Ugh this woman

frustrated me sometimes! I nodded. It was my job to remain silent, and pay attention. Not to ask questions. "Viperberry beetles contain the only anti-venom for a mercury viper bite in the world, but their poison is deadly if used wrong."

Honestly, banishing magic didn't sound like such a bad idea after all. Magic had been the bane of my existence, the one thing that would stop me from having a normal life, and the only thing that put Aggie in a foul temper around me. At least when I wasn't paying enough attention to it. Which was pretty much always.

We spent the next hour putting together the potion that would be the foundation for the Viperberry Hex with a complicated series of charms and enchantments, while my mind drifted to Glyn and what to do about him. There had to be a chance for us, somehow. But, like I'd been telling him for the past two years, it would be selfish of me to expect such a thing. He deserved a better life than I could give him. Aggie hissed at me for being lost in my thoughts.

"Pay attention, Jesobel! I've half a mind to send Starkeeper Yarrow a nyxiegram and tell her to find someone else! Unfortunately, there *isn't* anyone else. Your commitment to your duties is appalling. You should be ashamed of yourself, young lady." She shook her head at me with pursed lips and I shrank beneath her steely gaze, picturing her bony arm hurling a seething message sealed inside a bottle over the Cliffs of Rowan into the sea for the water nymphs to deliver. My great-grandmother would be ever so glad to hear what a failure I was. I shuddered, hugging myself.

"I'm sorry, Aggie," I whispered, and tried harder to focus.

When all of the ingredients were finally woven together and trapped inside the blue vial, and the final spell was cast upon the uncorked contents, I was made to memorize the words of the hex without weaving my quickflame with it. Quickflame would activate the hex and give me access to crazy strong Orphic magic, which I wasn't very good at controlling on my own, and which I needed to be able to prove I could at least somewhat safely weave into spells in just three days. I repeated the words a thousand times until I knew the incantation by heart. I mumbled that hex over and over and over as we made our way back to the Festival.

Beneath every word was a sense of foreboding that I couldn't shake, and by her silence, I knew Aggie felt it too. With the first hex out of the way, it meant I really was leaving in just a few short days. But what would happen if I wasn't truly prepared to take on my duties as Starkeeper? Because I wasn't. I knew it, and Aggie knew it. I glanced at her, confused as to why she continued to put such faith in me. And if she ever had plans to mention the Legend of Azimuth to me. I felt hopeless.

When the trees thinned and the gate came into view down the meadow, I returned to thoughts of Glyn, and my heart grew heavier in a different way. A decidedly more pleasant way than all of this hex nonsense. I couldn't wait to see him and forget about the disturbing words of Ethan Rowan taking root in the pit of my stomach.

CHAPTER 12

S eeing Glyn, it turned out, would have to wait yet another day. As we passed through the southern gate, over a hundred armored watchmen scurried around our marketplace like silver beetles, hammering notices to every signpost, tree trunk, and paddock fence in sight. My stomach dropped to my feet as we rounded the lane and a loose scroll fluttered across Pennyfeather's head and into my lap.

Aggie stopped next to me.

"What does it say, Jesobel?"

I scanned it a little, feeling sick to my stomach, and then read it aloud to her: "By Order of the Equulean Starkeeper, Ethan Rowan, any Pyxie found to be using magic of any sort shall be imprisoned immediately. Magic, and its use for any reason whatsoever, is hereby banished in the Realm of Equuleus forevermore."

"Well that was fast," I said, as Aggie yanked the scroll from my hands.

"We'll have to be very careful, Jesobel. You still have two hexes to learn," she whispered gravely.

My entire body ached with stress and lack of sleep. And lack of Glyn.

"What are we going to do?" I asked, thinking of that amulet and what a spectacle of magic it had made of me up on the hill just a day ago. I could feel its presence deep at the bottom of my gatherings bag, mocking me with its dark secrets. Did I dare tell Aggie about that amulet now? Part of me wanted to, but part of me wanted to spend my last few days not being scolded any more than usual.

"We're going to use caution. We're going to lie low. We'll have to pack up all the spell bottles; we could get arrested for selling those, now."

"But there's not even any real magic woven into them!"

"Ethan Rowan doesn't know that. We'd better hurry before one of his metal minions sees our stall!"

We hurried slowly, so as not to draw attention to ourselves, down our alleyway between two shoppe lanes, known among us Pyxies as Mystic Alley, named mainly for Aggie's spells. When we reached our campsite, Aggie rushed to the wagon and took out a small crate of herbal tinctures and essential oils.

"Quickly, replace the potions and charms with these, Jesobel."

The sun was sinking below the horizon, and a swath of billowy clouds stretched across the sky, all lit up in shades of reds and pinks and oranges. It made for an eerie scene, seeing those fiery colors reflected on the watchmen's shiny armor as they clumsily hammered away, making the whole marketplace sound as if it were being attacked by a flock of angry woodpeckers.

I removed all of the bottles I had spent so much time arranging and put the medicinals on the shelf. As I placed the last bottle of essential oil (rose geranium) on the tiered display, a watchman appeared with his hammer and scroll, eyeing our empty signpost with lust.

"What's all that?" he asked, using his hammer to point at my display. "That a bunch of hocus-pocus witchy potions?" His eagerness for me to say yes was disturbing. An arrest on the first day might bring him some sort of special bonus from Rowan.

"Nope, just essential oils," I said, backing up into the crate full of potions and enchantments at my feet. I could feel my heart starting to race. Where was Aggie?

"What's the point o' that?" he said, his hammer drooping.

"They just smell good," I explained, nudging the crate behind me a smidgen at a time to the other side of the scarf wall.

"You sure them aren't spells and whatnot? Looks an awful lot like *magic* to me." He shifted anxiously, his armor making metallic clicks and clacks. So eager to arrest me! My heart thumped in my chest so hard I feared he could hear it.

"Do you have a wife?" I asked, stepping toward him while giving the crate of phony spells a final heel-shove backward and out of sight. "Here, smell this, tell me what you think." I grabbed a bottle from the shelf and uncorked it, cramming it toward his nose.

He gave me a funny look, almost as if he were afraid for a second. Afraid I might hex him or something.

"Go on, smell it!" I urged, smiling as big as I could manage.

He leaned in, his empty hand holding his helmet's shield up. "Hm. Smells pretty good. Do you have any moonblossom? My wife does love moonblossom."

Not moonblossom! I hadn't seen any in that crate. "I'm not sure, let me ask my Guardian."

I ran behind the scarves and found Aggie sitting on the stairs with her elbows on her knees and her head in her hands. It worried me to see her like that. "Aggie, are you okay?" I whispered, gently touching her shoulder, since she probably didn't hear me.

"What?" Her head shot up like a gopher coming out of its hole. "Jessa, don't sneak up on me like that!" She let out a heavy sigh and looked at me, waiting.

"Oh, there's a watchman in the shoppe. He's looking for moonblossom essential oil. Do we have any? He's making me nervous," I added.

"Did you put everything away?"

I nodded.

"I might have a bottle in the cupboard. Just give it to him and get him out of here!"

I squeezed past her and ran to the cupboard in the back of the wagon and dug through Aggie's personal stash. The moonblossom was all the way in the back and looked about a million years old, all crusted with gunk, and the cork looked chewed on. I fished around for a clean empty bottle, and just before I was about to give up, found one with a single dried leaf inside it. "That'll work," I said aloud, rushing as fast as I could. I dumped the leaf onto the breakfast table, which was still folded down, and carefully poured the moonblossom oil into the new bottle. I popped the cork in place and jumped off the top stair, and ran to the scarf wall, swiping the colorful silks out of the way. The watchman was there; he had hammered a notice onto our signpost and was just turning around when I reached him.

"Here," I said. "Take it. For your wife." I hoped I didn't look too terribly nervous or sweaty. He uncorked the bottle and inhaled.

"That's the stuff! How much do I owe you?"

"It's okay, you can have it." I smiled, attempting to look younger and more innocent than I actually was.

"You sure?"

"I'm sure. Just bring your wife back and buy her another on Everday!"

He walked away sniffing the dainty bottle, stars peeking from the fading pink sky behind him, as his metal legs scraped awkwardly together in a scene that was almost comical.

I exhaled heavily, not realizing I had been holding my breath.

"That was close," I said to no one in particular.

Aggie poked her head through the scarves. "Are you going to the Quickfire tonight?"

"I don't think so. I'm pretty beat." I wasn't ready to face all those people. Not after that complete debacle of exploding the Quickfire into a towering inferno last night. Nope, I was ready for some good sleep.

"I'm going to go to bed early, I think." And wait for Glyn to knock on my berth floor...

Surely he would come tonight, wouldn't he?

CHAPTER 13

I lay in the dark, unable to sleep, my mind a tumble of red hair and that not-so-secret kiss between Glyn and Seraphina Bellamy. Fuming, I blinked away the image of strawberry lips pressed against Glyn's smiling mouth. The pressure in my chest had been constant since the Quickfire, and was now rife with a senseless fury that felt like metal grinding against rock.

The world outside the wagon was still and perfectly silent. I couldn't see any light eking in through the crack in my berth doors, and then my eyes adjusted and the pale glow of seven nearly full moons made a ghostly glowing stripe between them. When I couldn't stand the claustrophobic feeling inside my body or my berth any longer, I slid the doors open as quietly as I could and crawled out of the wagon.

When I slipped through the smallest possible crack in the front door and pushed it into place behind me, I drew a huge, crisp breath into my lungs. It was unusually warm outside for the end of Maple Moon, but there was still a deep chill in the air. I turned my face upward to drink in the magic of the dark sky. The stars fought to stay bright in the wake of the moonglow. Three of the moons had already set, while the four smallest moons would be faintly visible through mid-morning. There wasn't a cloud to be seen. As I sucked cool air into my lungs, I wished I could breathe in the entire expanse of the sky to make the tight pressure leave my chest.

I briefly considered sneaking through the marketplace to throw pebbles at Glyn's window, but decided against it when Firefly stepped around the corner and nuzzled me.

"Hey, boy, what are you doing here?" I whispered in his ear. The pressure in my chest lessened at the sight of my horse, as if at least one of the five thousand anvils stacked on it had been removed. Firefly always made everything more bearable. It was so quiet that my whisper sounded like a yell in the stillness of the night.

"Hey, what do you say we get out of here and go for a ride?" I slipped on my boots and pulled my wool cloak from the hook outside the door, and as an afterthought grabbed my bow and quiver and slung them onto my back. I needed to practice shooting from horseback. Glyn had been practicing. I couldn't let him get better than me. Firefly nickered low and his kind eyes glittered in affirmation.

I led him down Mystic Alley, careful to step lightly around campfires and cookstoves, and tried not to make a racket in the sprawling, sleepy marketplace. As soon as we stepped into Tinker's Lane, I hopped onto his back, and even though we both wanted to gallop—I could feel that twitch in Firefly's muscles—we walked to the northeast gate so none of the other horses got any ideas to follow us. All we needed was a stampede of flirty mares chasing Firefly down the lane at this hour. Aggie would just love that.

As soon as we were through the gate Firefly broke into a gallop toward the borders of the forest. His powerful muscles moved in a rhythm beneath my seat in a way that felt like all was right in the universe. I sank into it and listened to the cadence of his hoof beats thrumming on the soft clover while the cool air kissed my cheeks. We stayed close to the wall until the trees grew more and more dense, and then we eased into the forest, staying parallel to the wall. We threaded through the black tree trunks until what little pale moonlight lighting our way was mostly blocked out by the canopy, and a starless darkness surrounded us. I summoned my illumins, bracing myself for their ticklish pop, and let Liliet and her family light the way.

Soon, the wild tangle of trees forced us to slow. As quiet space gathered between each decelerated hoof beat, I listened to the slumbering forest. Only the crunching of dried leaves underfoot and the occasional skittering off of some small creature in the undergrowth joined Firefly's puffed exhales. My spark fairies floated along, dancing in the charming way they do, and Firefly didn't question where we were going, he just faithfully continued forward.

But as I was starting to wonder exactly what my plan was, a tingling sensation at the base of my skull triggered an unwelcome alertness that stiffened my spine. We were being watched. I mostly wanted to just take a relaxing ride and fire off some arrows into tree stumps, but a sense that we were not alone with the creatures of the forest began to nag at me.

My illumins answered to unspoken commands. They were part of me, part of my quickflame. They made a wide circle around me and my horse, and I tried to act natural as I peered between and beyond them for any signs of followers. I cursed myself for not making a windowroot charm upon entering the woods. Aggie would chide me for being so careless, and for once I would have to agree.

When I was a small child, the adults and teenagers would tell frightening stories around the campfire. Tales of ghosts and ghouls that haunted marshes and lakes, tales of ugly mud sprites that stole children and whisked them underground to live as slaves, forced to dig endless tunnels far beneath the loamy vale. On many occasions, the adults would go to bed, leaving the kids to ruminate over these tales around the dying cookfire. When the last embers would lose their glow, we would leave the comforting ring of light and warmth and cross the expanse of darkness toward our wagons for the night. There wasn't a single one of us who didn't run for our lives, stricken faster and faster with a prickly, spine-tingling sensation of being pursued by a gruesome mud sprite or malevolent ghost or ghoul. I remember never looking back, and my heart would hammer in my chest for long minutes after I slammed my berth doors shut and lay listening for the imagined squadgy footsteps of a nasty mud sprite closing in.

I felt like that now. I wanted to urge Firefly to run, but there were too many trees, too close together, and so I was forced to move slowly with what I hoped was irrational fear building inside of me until my hands began to quake. An eerie sound, though faint and far off, zapped me from the base of my skull to my stomach like a bolt of lightning. Firefly's muscles tensed beneath me, and he stopped, frozen, his ears rotating this way and that to find the direction of the sound, which was something like an ethereal howl, rising in crescendo and coming from everywhere and nowhere all at once.

The illumins gathered close and shivered in a way I'd never seen them do. Their tiny wings vibrated, they refused to venture from between Firefly's ears, and some clung to his mane. Something was wrong. Something was very, very wrong. The howl was answered by another, this one much closer. The sound didn't grow audibly louder, but I sensed it as louder... its coldness spread through me like an icy shadow. I reached for my bow and nocked an arrow, but something inside of me knew that this weapon would do no good against whatever was stalking us. I sensed Orphic magic, dark and dangerous. The second howl was answered by a third and a fourth, until the coldness of the wailing caused my bow to quiver violently in my quaking hands, the arrow rattling noisily against it.

Firefly's hooves made small, nervous steps and his ears twitched in every direction. He nickered low and throaty, arching his neck, and I felt his muscles changing and preparing for takeoff; he was just waiting for my cue.

I needed to know what was out there. The spark fairies went dark at my request, and once my eyes adjusted I scanned the forest for signs of what could be making those horrible sounds. I heard no rustle of leaves, nor any footsteps, but the electric fear that lit up my spine told me whatever they were, they were dangerously close. Out of the corner of my eye, I glimpsed a flash of light. I whipped my head toward the source and saw two hot, white eyes blink with a frightening intensity, framed by the shape of a wolfish shadow. The air began to crackle with devilsflare. I was not prepared to combat it. Immediately, I was consumed by every dark thought I'd ever had, every sadness; every anguished moment of my life was magnified and took hold of my heart, squeezing. I felt as though my soul was being sucked into a state of despair, and it was all I could do to keep from bursting into racking sobs.

"Firefly," I squeaked, slinging my bow back in place and returning the arrow to the quiver. "*Run.*"

Firefly spun around and raced through the trees, and I did what I could to hunker down and stay safe from low branches. I hung on tight to a fistful of mane, but my sense of self-preservation waned with every thunderous step. The cold shadow-creatures were at our heels in an instant, surrounding us on all sides and coming after us with mournful, baleful wails and howls that hurled me into deeper and deeper states of despair. There was an abyss of darkness sucking me downward, end every horrifying emotion swirled within it. I was being sucked into the Orphic!

I struggled to call my illumins to help Firefly find his way, but their light dimmed and waned as despair took root in my consciousness, blocking out my ability to connect with my own quickflame, to weave Mystic magic from anything around me, and even my desire to do so.

Instead, I imagined satisfying scenes of being raked from my seat by a tremendous claw and dragged into the Orphic to become a feast for the creatures. They could rip me from limb to limb, and I would welcome them. Anything to stop the vat of dark emotion that boiled inside of my heart and mind, reminding me that I was unworthy. Unworthy of Glyn, unworthy of becoming Starkeeper. Unworthy of calling myself a faithful Pyxie. Unworthy to be Aggie's apprentice. Unworthy to care for my beautiful horse, whose life was now in utter danger. Unworthy to *live*.

Cold wolfish breath and icy spittle found my flesh as we dashed through the trees, and it burned where it landed. I screamed out and remembered all of the times I'd disappointed Aggie, and shame welled up in my heart. I looked left and saw flashes of wicked rows of teeth and blinks of rough, black devilsflare fur. Long bruise-colored tongues foaming with vile black slobber lapped at the air, tasting my suffering. They howled and groaned and yipped for more, frenzied like sharks drawn to blood.

My mind was slammed with the image of Glyn's hurt expression when I left him at the gate. I was suddenly so sorry for ignoring him that I felt I deserved to die. I considered letting go of Firefly, letting my body slip and tumble to the ground. Allowing the beasts to have me and do what they would, so that my horse could escape. I imagined my death would come fast; there must have been a dozen of them growling at my heels. The thought of death soothed me. The expanding pain that bloomed in every cell of my being would stop if I just let them take me and end my suffering. I led my beloved horse into this mess! I hated myself with fierce intensity. He would die unless I did something to save him. Firefly doesn't deserve to die! *I do, I do, I do*.

I was about to release my grip on Firefly's mane when I noticed a pale light seeping between the trees up ahead. My poor illumins were nothing but ghostly dying fireflies, clinging to my horse's ears and forelock like a wilting crown of day-old blossoms. It was my fault they were dying. They looked to me with sad tiny eyes, and I saw their small mouths moving, their tiny faces twisted in imploring shapes. Liliet's wee pregnant belly bounced against my horse as she clung to a handful of hair. They reached out to me, begged me to do something, but I could no longer hear them or feel them. I was numb to them. My poor little spark fairies! Liliet's baby! Another wave of shame added to the last, and I was so filled with misery and self-loathing that I knew finally what I must do.

I wasn't going to simply let go of Firefly and tumble backwards so he had a chance to flee; I was going to scan the gnashing pack of doom that licked at our heels and fling myself at the scariest-looking one in the bunch.

As I carefully considered each of the dozen hounds, looking for a spark of recognition that said, *Yes, this is the one who will end your misery*, Firefly began to zig and zag like he was cutting cattle through the thinning trees. The spark fairies screamed out in silence and hung onto strands of forelock and mane, some flailing and whipping about at the end of tiny horsehair ropes. An orange ray of early morning sunlight bathed the forest floor about fifty yards ahead, yet the beauty of it was lost on me as I searched for the wolfish specter I would sacrifice myself to.

I felt nothing but doom and despair pulling me down, down, down. The eerie lamenting of the wolves rang out louder, and I sensed them closing in, working together to tighten the circle they'd made around us. Firefly kicked out, a pained yelp squealed behind me, and a wolf stumbled and fell behind. A low bone-rattling growl, deeper than a rumble of thunder, gained in volume until the curled grimace of every hound culminated in an ear-splitting guttural siren.

It was now or never; they were about to attack. The place in my chest where my quickflame lived was a vacuum of despair, turning in on itself endlessly, dragging all happiness from my heart, from my memories, and replacing it with a sodden blanket of shame and sorrow.

I hated myself so fiercely and all that I held onto was my horse. His safety. I could save him if I sacrificed myself. The largest wolf edged next to me until his cold breath beckoned me to follow him. I locked eyes with the creature—his were white with pale orange electricity webbing across the surface. An image flashed in my mind. My mother's spent face smiling weakly at me, and then taking her final breath.

My entire being was jolted by a horrible realization, an awful truth. *I killed my mother.* I screamed out, a fiery sob ripping through my lungs. I could not bear the thought of my birth taking my mother's life. I had killed her!

I looked at the wolf. A black tongue licked across its hideous toothy grin, his nose quivering at the scent of my anguish. His eyes crackled with orange light, beckoning me toward his dark maw, a deep abyss of nothingness lined with jagged ebony teeth; a promise of quick relief from this intense suffering. I imagined what those wicked teeth would feel like ripping into my flesh, as I swung my leg around Firefly's neck and leapt toward his snapping jaws.

CHAPTER 14

Perhaps I saved my horse, I heard myself think, the thought sounding far, far outside my body. *And my sweet little illumins will be free again. My dear and faithful spark fairies. Liliet can have her baby and they can live happily in the Mystic when I'm gone.*

I sank into an abyss of fathomless sorrow and waited for teeth to crunch through muscle and bone and sweep away the puddle of shame that was me, lying there on the forest floor, and replace my body with a smear of blood and guts. I wished it would happen faster.

Instead, I felt Firefly's muzzle push on my cheek with a blast of grass-scented breath, and a robin's song rang out, a strange juxtaposition to the cacophony of frustrated whines, yips and barks echoing, still too near. Why had I decided a midnight ride to the forest was a good idea?

"Firefly, get back!" I leaped up, tried to ready myself to fight the Orphic wolves away from my horse, ready to sacrifice myself again. Death appealed to me, but I didn't know why. I quickly scanned the ground for my bow, while sliding an arrow from the cockeyed quiver on my back.

I shoved Firefly's rump. "Go!" I shouted. Firefly didn't budge. He lowered his head and found a tuft of grass.

"What's wrong with you!" I shrieked at my stupid horse. "Get out of here!" I scooped up my bow, whipping toward the eerie hound-song, ready to take down as many as I could, instinctively tipping my arrows with crackling quickflame—magic I learned long ago and didn't realize until now that I had even remembered.

I stood there, my body as taught as my bowstring for an awkward moment in which Firefly wandered in front of me, methodically pulling up tufts of grass poking up from the leaf-scattered ground, and chewing them without a care in the world. The hound-song rose in frustrated crescendo from where they now gathered, a writhing mass of shadows just beyond the soft beam of sunlight between us, which they were apparently unable to cross. I fired a few shots anyway, and landed all three. After a moment of screeching yowls and whines, whimpers and frustrated barks, they turned, defeated, and slunk into the forest, reptilian and Orphic.

I sighed and turned to Firefly, heavy with relief. My handsome, brilliant stallion wore a twinkling crown of spark fairies who were busy singing in their silent voices and dancing happily around his ears. Liliet cuddled his lucky white ear, her legs crossed beneath her pregnant stomach, with a huge smile on her teensy face.

Finally, the agonizing pull of darkness released its hold and drained from my body, out my feet and down deep into the ground, back to the Orphic where it belonged. The devilsflare seeped away with it, but something tugged at the icy circle where the compass had been. There was a crawly sensation beneath my skin, as if the needle were spinning there.

A lightness of being overwhelmed me, and my heart pulsed with love for my dear companions. But my stomach tightened when I realized exactly how angry Aggie would be when I told her what happened.

We took our time returning to the gate, Firefly following the steep downward slope with hip-swiveling steps. The pastel colors of the sunrise fanned across the morning sky, washing out the remaining moons with pale, newborn daylight.

When the gate drew near, comforting smells of breakfast wafting from vendors' booths gave my stomach a reason to growl. In minutes, hunger trumped my fear of facing Aggie. I needed to eat, and my gatherings bag was in the wagon with her. I urged Firefly into a trot and turned down Savory Lane, lined on either side with vendors selling fragrant Pyxie dishes from around the world, stalls boasting colorful spices and herbs, sugars and salts, and booths bursting with fresh local vegetables and exotic fruits transported from far-off places.

"Jessa! Think fast!" Franci flashed a warm, freckle-nosed grin and tossed me a gooey cinnamon bun as we trotted by her bakery. I snatched it out of the air and bit into the hot dough, letting the steam warm my fingers and face. Sticky icing dripped down my hand.

"Thanks, Franshi," I managed. The comfort of hot sugary cinnamon bread heating my belly awoke me to the present, and the drama of my late night adventure took a back seat. I breathed deeply and relaxed for the first time in what felt like forever, and just enjoyed the familiarity of the marketplace.

Being without a stationary home meant that many things and places could fill my heart with a sense of home. This colorful marketplace, the one place where so many Pyxians from around the world gathered each year, was home in a grand way. Sure, our traveling caravan shrank or expanded in numbers throughout the year as families joined up with us for a leg and then split off to some other destination, and that had its own sense of home. This was different. This almost felt permanent, especially since it was the place where I was born.

As we ambled past the quaint wooden signs swinging happily from tar-scented posts, I delighted in the comforting hum of sweatered and hatted bodies at work all around me as the sun rose, not yet warming anyone's bones. The smoke from cookfires at the food vendor's booths curled up lazily in some places, and billowed in hot bursts in others.

Vegetables sizzled on iron grills, pots bubbled and boiled and the array of sweet and savory scents mingled together to create a vague, ancient memory of the Lost Realm of Pyxis—a nostalgia that existed in our very cells, since actual memories of our homeland had long since been extinct. This fleeting, temporary marketplace gave me a sense of home like no place else I had ever traveled.

When I reluctantly reached Aggie's wagon, the sun was still low and the sky was pale yellow fading into light blue. The stars went back to the Mystic until the moonrise, when they would return to balance the Orphic energy of the night with their Mystic light. The moons had traveled across the sky, and disappeared on the horizon like fat dolphins diving into the sea.

A new paper leaflet was nailed to our signpost. I tore it down and read it as I dismounted from Firefly, and sent him to graze.

"Jesobel. Where have you been?" Aggie stood rigid, fists balled on her slender hips, and glared at me. Her tight angry curls vibrated like a swarm of bees were hiding in there.

"Aggie, I'm sorry. I tried to make it back in time." I half-listened to her, reading the leaflet with a sinking sensation. Aggie must not have seen this yet.

"Just what exactly did you feel a need to do all night long? Couldn't you have at least gotten back here at a decent hour? You know what we have to do today. The Second Venom." Her gaze was deadly. I couldn't even look directly at her. I crumpled the paper in my hand.

Where did she think I was all night? With Glyn? It wasn't the first time I'd taken a morning walk alone!

"I got up early, Aggie. I couldn't sleep. But I was here all night, I promise. I just went for a ride with Firefly, that's all."

But that wasn't all, and I wanted to tell her about what happened in the forest, but I wasn't sure if I should. Guilt began its weighty descent into the pit of my stomach, making a rock-like mess of the cinnamon bun, and I was annoyed that she hinted I was off with Glyn. I wanted to cry all of a sudden, so I bit my lip until I tasted the coppery tang of blood, and tried to focus on that. And then I remembered the paper in my hand.

"Aggie, have you seen this?"

"What is it," she snapped. "We don't have time for nonsense this morning."

"Ethan Rowan is not only banishing magic from Equuleus, but beginning on Quickbane..." I smoothed the crumpled paper and handed it to her. "...it is punishable by death," I whispered.

"Oh dear." Her voice was far too grave so early in the morning. "I secretly summoned the bleakhounds last night. We need to get to the forest immediately. The longer they roam in our world, the hungrier they get. The hungrier they get, the more difficult they are to work with, and the more solid they become. If they aren't controlled immediately, they could wreak havoc on everything. Everyone. If Rowan finds out I've summoned Orphic creatures, we will all be put to death! For now, they are trapped in the woods—I placed an enchantment to keep them there, but I don't know how long that will last. If they find the perimeter..."

I almost swallowed my heart. It dropped into my boots. Bleakhounds? Is that what those were?! For the love of Ariah, what had I done? I thought it was the sunlight trapping them in the forest. But it was Aggie's enchantment. And they *did* find the perimeter. I led them right to it.

My insides felt wobbly. I avoided eye contact and helped Aggie pack things, grabbing random items and shoving them into my gatherings bag. I didn't know what I needed to bring. Maybe nothing. I knew I should tell Aggie what I had done, but she would kill me for going to the forest alone in the first place, so I bit my tongue. Maybe we'd get there in time. Maybe their magic wouldn't draw attention to us. Maybe we wouldn't be executed.

How did my life get so horrible so fast? I wanted to crawl into my berth and cry my eyes out until I went numb. And then I wanted to turn back time, or nominate someone else to take my place. Why not that stupid redhead? She should be the Starkeeper. Then I could stay home with Glyn. Why did I have to do this? Why did I have to get tangled up in all sorts of annoying magic? I didn't want to go back to that forest. I didn't want to see those bleakhounds ever again.

Like a fool, I stumbled onto the lane and scanned the line of stalls, desperately hoping to see Glyn. As if Aggie would even give me three seconds with him. But of course, he was nowhere.

"Time to go. Penny's grazing. Go get her and meet me at the gate," she whisper-yelled at me, which was the worst. Usually her voice was so loud, and that high volume actually comforted me. When she went quiet, it was as if she had the power to make the whole universe vanish with a single command. For such a tiny woman, Aggie could strike fear into me like nothing else when she was angry. Those orange-eyed bleakhounds had nothing on her.

I nodded and took off around the wagon and into the lane to retrieve the mare. I was so hungry; that cinnamon bun had only made my hungrier. But there was no chance I could stop for food. I hoped Aggie had packed something. This day was going to be long and horrible, I just knew it. I could feel it in my bones. Hunger was not going to help it go by any quicker.

I found Pennyfeathers between a cluster of mares huddled shoulder to shoulder. "Come on, Penny, let's go." I swung myself onto her broad back and my boot heel came down on something with a disturbing thwap as I settled into my seat.

"Ow!"

"Oh no! Glyn! What are you doing here?" I had kicked the boy I loved square in the ear. "Oh, gosh, I'm so sorry! Are you okay?"

He held his red-hot ear and smiled up at me. His smile hurt my heart. "Hey, Jessa. I'm so happy to see you." There was something sad and serious behind the twinkle in his eyes. I didn't want to hear about that stupid girl.

"Hey, how 'bout a morning ride? Come to the lake with me?"

Had my luck just taken a turn for the worst that it would never recover from? Part of me wanted to say yes and take off down the meadow in the opposite direction, hoping against hope that nothing was going on between Glyn and Seraphina, that I was imagining the whole thing. Part of me wanted to ride all the way to the sea wall and look at the ocean and let Glyn's easy smile wash away all of my heartache and fear, even if my stomach did feel tight and queasy when I looked at him.

Instead, I got Penny to put a few steps between us and I forced myself to speak. "I can't. I have to go with Aggie. I'm so sorry about your ear." And I urged Pennyfeathers into a gallop without looking back, leaving him there, holding his ear with that same dejected look I left him with yesterday. Only worse.

My heart cracked inside my chest, the gaping chasm between the two halves like the opening to the Orphic, dark and fathomless. A few tears escaped and flew off my cheeks into the wind as we galloped toward Aggie. And those bleakhounds.

A scream boiled up inside of me that I was not allowed to let out.

CHAPTER 15

ggie looked fierce. She wrapped a green scarf over her head and knotted it at the nape of her neck, covering her silver halo of curls. Every wrinkle on her face seemed to be frowning individually, and I couldn't help but feel sorry that this ugly facial contortion was my fault. She arched a disapproving eyebrow, despite the speed with which I made it to the gate. I shriveled under the sharp intensity of that glare.

She tapped Firefly with her heel, and they sprang forward like they'd been shot from a bow, galloping through the huge gate and up the sloping hill toward the forest, sage skirts, feathered feet, miles of mane and tail flying. I hadn't seen Aggie ride like that since... ever. Like her whispery voice, this ferocious speed unnerved me completely.

I inhaled one last tantalizing whiff of savory market food. There was something garlicky and oniony and mouthwateringly rosemary-ish floating on the breeze. I hoped the scent would somehow sustain me until this awful day was over. Then I rode after Aggie, a heavy dread gathering in every cell of my body, doubling or maybe even tripling my actual weight with its leaden pressure.

Even though Pennyfeathers was the one doing all the running, I was breathless when we caught up to Aggie and Firefly at the edge of the woods. I scanned the trees for some sign of the bleakhounds, and hoped to Ariah that they found something else to interest themselves with so I could keep my little adventure a secret. Even though I felt horrible for having such a secret in the first place.

Aggie was kneeling, busy digging through her bag, pulling out little shreds of herbs and papers and vials of this and that, waving things around her head and saying magical words that I should've probably been paying attention to, but she didn't even notice me there, so I just sat and waited, and kept my eyes out for the bleakhounds while daydreaming about Glyn, trying to solve our predicament.

It didn't take long for them to sniff us out. I felt them approach before I saw or heard them, their dark magic sweeping across me like a cold mist, smothering my quickflame. I looked at Aggie, hoping she would conjure some hex and make them go away, but she didn't seem to notice their arrival. She just kept fussing with her spell.

I managed to summon my spark fairies in an effort to keep them safe. They popped free, but this time it didn't tickle. I could feel their pain—they were already suffering under the bleakhounds' evil appetites. I must have let some sort of noise escape from my increasingly sorrowful lips because Aggie shot me a look that could reduce boulders to dust.

"Jesobel!" she barked with deeply frowning brows. "Are you even paying attention?" Her disappointment in me was a stab to my soul.

I tried to nod, but my body was molasses, moving in slow motion. There was a sensation in my chest that felt like someone dropped me off a cliff and my lungs got stuck in that moment—breathless and unable to suck in enough air to survive. My eyes were saucers; I could feel them magnifying the terror that had crept wolf-like into the center of my quickflame, readying itself to feed on me with black fangs and poisonous saliva. I tried to locate the bleakhounds, but the surrounding trees were empty of the howling wolves. I didn't understand. I gasped for air.

Why hadn't Aggie stopped them? Why didn't she feel them, too?

Why couldn't I see them? They were so close I could feel their icy breath chilling the back of my neck!

Firefly grazed calmly and Penny was unconcerned beneath my seat, enjoying mouthfuls of sweet spring grass. But my spark fairies wilted and writhed in pain.

"Aggie," I managed to croak. But it came out too quietly. She wouldn't hear me unless I yelled. Damn that deaf woman! I could feel panic rising, as my quickflame began to dim and the overwhelming sorrow, the absolute bleakness overcame me.

I am going to die on the back of Penny, and Aggie is so furious with me she won't even notice until I fall to the ground with a thud.

For some reason, this idea stirred up some fight in me. Maybe because Aggie already had to watch my mother die. Maybe because I felt responsible for that. And maybe I couldn't bear the thought of putting Aggie through so much pain again. I'd already disappointed her so deeply. I tried to call out again, but my voice was nothing, a scratchy wisp of a thing, useless upon nearly deaf ears.

Aggie continued on with her spell, confident that I was rapt with attention, memorizing every herb and charm that went into that second Hex. I focused on a pinprick of light, imagining it in my chest like a tiny spark fairy. I flicked my eyes around the landscape and saw a plant I could call on. It was just a vine of some sort, with ruddy purplish leaves twining up the trunk of a dead tree. If I didn't remember its name, I wouldn't be able to summon its quickflame. I thought about summoning the quickflame from a tree instead, but there was no way of telling how deep or dark their roots might be. Plus, with the bleakhounds near, they could encourage the trees to summon Orphic magic, persuade them to absorb devilsflare.

My hopes were dashed as my eyes scanned for a safe plant to use, and settled back on the nondescript vine whose name I couldn't recall. I was beginning to sag under the weight of agony and despair that licked at me from hungry, poisonous tongues.

When I turned to Aggie to give her a silent goodbye and a woeful apology, whether she could hear me or not, it popped into my mind. Woodbine! The moment I heard the name echo through my mind, the lighter I began to feel. I summoned the little plant's magic. It reached out to me, combining with my quickflame, strengthening me. I stoked the flame against the bleakhounds' dark magic until my chest was vibrating like leaves in a breeze—surging with current after current of white-hot magic.

My heart flooded with thoughts of everyone I loved. Of Aggie, of Fin and Myriam. Of Glyn. Of my beloved Firefly. I remembered happy moments, dancing with Glyn around the fire, or galloping free with Firefly, and I felt soothing strands of quickflame weaving together from each of them. The compass flared to life beneath my chest, the needle spinning steadily, not wildly like before, until it looped and slowed to a shaky wiggle, wavering back and forth between two points. I began to sing, Firefly's song, my mother's song, and suddenly there was a sound that rang out through my chest. A piercing musical howl and a pack of wolves the color of starlight leapt from the Mystic, gleaming with pure quickflame, and charged into the trees, disappearing into the dark canopy after the bleakhounds. I heard the yips and whimpers of the bleakhounds as they retreated with tails between their legs, the Mystic creatures bellowing after them, and I was released from their hungry feeding frenzy. My illumins wriggled with joy.

Aggie stood up and glared at me, holding up a large, black, fang-shaped crystal dangling from a length of leather.

"Were you even paying attention?" She shouted, when she saw me still astride Penny. "Get down from there and act like you care about becoming our Starkeeper, Jesobel! Honestly, Starkeeper Yarrow is going to be sorely disappointed at your meager progress. She'll certainly have her work cut out for her, trying to get anything to sink into your thick head. How do you think that makes me look, huh?"

I guess I hadn't thought of that.

Aggie stomped around in a small circle to let off her steam and I slid down and walked a few steps to lean against Firefly. I couldn't believe that entire bleakhound episode took place without her even noticing.

"Here. The Bleakhound Hex." She held the smooth crystal out to me, and I reached for it. "Ah, ah, ah," she tutted, pulling it from my grasp.

"Your turn," she said, waving her hand over the crystal until it burst into a purple flame and vanished. "I certainly hope you meant it when you said you were paying attention."

She wasn't even attempting to be civil anymore. I tried not to roll my eyes. Or panic. I didn't see a single thing she did to make that hex. I really missed the old Aggie, the Aggie that wasn't so obsessed with turning me into something I didn't even want to be.

"Into the woods we go," declared Aggie, gathering up her supplies and clucking to Firefly. She marched into the trees and I reluctantly followed behind the horses, keeping a wary eye out for more of those frightful bleakhounds.

I should have been exhausted and hungry, but I felt energized. As we walked by the woodbine, I whispered a blessing of gratitude. The leaves shimmered as I passed.

As we got deeper into the woods, Aggie began to fidget, looking around with a perplexed expression contorting her wrinkly old face.

"What's wrong, Aggie?" I shouted, so she would hear me on the first try.

"Nothing… yet," she said. But I could tell it was something huge. I scanned our surroundings but I could neither feel nor see any bleakhounds, or anything else that might be a threat to us. Aggie became visibly stressed, though her silence attempted to hide it.

"I don't understand," she mumbled, spinning circles in a small clearing, scanning the trees beyond with concerned eyes.

"What is it, Aggie?" She was making me nervous, though I perceived no threat.

"The bleakhounds. They're gone. This can only mean one thing. The perimeter. They've breached it." Aggie managed to nimbly swing herself onto Firefly's back and was already threading through the trees when she shouted back at me in a voice thick with terror, "Hurry, there's no time to lose! They'll be at the marketplace any minute!"

I grabbed a fistful of Penny's mane at her withers and slipped onto her back, urging her after Firefly while the cinnamon bun in my stomach tried to change its mind about being digested. Not because the bleakhounds were about to wreak havoc on the entire marketplace, their magic drawing enough attention for Rowan to have any number of Pyxies put to death. No. I was sick to the point of seeing the world spin before me because the opposite was true.

The bleakhounds were gone, but not to the marketplace. They went back to the Orphic where they belonged. I knew, because I sent them there, with the help of that woodbine. With the help of those starlight-colored wolves. Only one Pyxie would face certain death today, and that Pyxie was me. When Aggie killed me after I told her about the run-in I had with those bleakhounds that morning, and how they came for me again.

I took a deep breath when Penny was galloping down the grassy slope toward the marketplace alongside Firefly. "Aggie!" I had to scream at the top of my lungs so she'd hear me above the thrumming hoofbeats beneath us. "Aggie, stop! Wait!"

"There's no time, Jesobel! We must hurry!" I'd never seen her apricot face so determined and concerned. As we neared the wall and the big metal gate, it occurred to me that we were quite a spectacle. There would be questions from the guards, magic or no, and that was

⋙ 108 ⋘

the last thing we needed. I had no choice. I led Penny into a big arc closing in around Firefly's muzzle, causing him to turn as well. As we passed by, I grabbed a hank of his long mane, and dragged him back up the hill toward the woods with Aggie shouting every angry curse she could think of at me. I led the horse until we crested the hill, rising, and then falling out of view from any guards posted at the gate. Aggie was in hysterics, mad as a badger, and doing all she could to turn my horse around and go back to the stalls.

"Aggie, STOP!" I slipped off Penny's back and pulled Aggie off Firefly's back.

"The bleakhounds are gone, Aggie. They've gone back to the Orphic."

"How do you know?" Aggie was frantic, pushing at me, but I held her shoulders tight.

"Because I sent them back," I said. "I sent them back where they belong."

"What do you mean, Jesobel? How?"

"I... I don't know. I summoned magic from a vine. A woodbine vine. I just... sang. And there were these white wolves..." I was suddenly embarrassed. "That's all. I swear."

"Brighthounds? That's impossible." Aggie glared at me, and pushed my hands from her shoulders. She spun toward the forest, and then toward the marketplace. All was quiet. She grabbed me by the shoulders and scanned me from head to toe. It was as if she was seeing me for the first time, and I couldn't tell if she liked what she saw. In fact, I could see that she didn't.

"We need to get back in there and you need to learn that Hex, immediately," said Aggie. Her voice was so serious. I was dizzy with the apprehension in her eyes. "It's getting late, and we still have to come back here tonight for the final Hex. The ghostmoths will only appear at midnight for a short time. And you. You are not leaving my side until then, understand?"

There was something Aggie wasn't telling me. But there was no way I was going to ask her what it was. I went silently back into the forest, leading Penny and Firefly beside me. Aggie followed behind, mumbling spells and enchantments I'd never heard of, and dousing me in protective magic. Her behavior made me anxious. I vowed to learn the Bleakhound Hex with rapt attention and no complaints. And I would not think of Glyn.

CHAPTER 16

The sun had gone down and a haze of purple twilight hung low over the marketplace, the blaze of the Quickfire cutting lively dancing shapes into the darkness as we passed through the gate on horseback. Merry music rang out, yet to my exhausted ear it sounded mournful, and was a reminder that I would soon be leaving as plain old Jesobel Vine for the last time. Next year, if I made it back by then, I would be a completely different person, or at least people would treat me differently. I would be their Starkeeper. And depending on how the Legend of Azimuth played out, I could either be on a path of destruction, or leading them all back to our Lost Realm. I still couldn't fathom that.

My stomach was so empty that it felt like it was digesting itself, and the smells of roasting potatoes and grilled vegetables floating on a breeze tortured me. There was no way I was asking Aggie if we could stop and grab a bite from a vendor. It was back to the wagon for us.

"Jesobel, you did a fine job learning that hex. I am proud of you." I was astonished to hear this, as Aggie hadn't spoken a word since we packed everything up and she draped the dark, tooth-shaped crystal around my neck. I could feel the hex—the devilsflare from the bleakhound's bite trapped inside felt so cold that it burned against my skin, reminding me of the compass. First chance I got, I was taking it off. I didn't like it.

"Thanks Aggie," I shouted, so she could hear me.

"You almost seemed like a real Magic Weaver today. So focused," she said, her scratchy, gravelly voice almost showing hints of warmth for the first time in ages. "Have you finally decided to take yourself seriously, Jesobel?" Her lips were pursed. I didn't even have to see her face to know it. So much for that warmth. "Have you finally decided to strive toward your destined potential?" She couldn't hide the condescending tone if she tried.

I let out a sigh that I knew she couldn't hear and wondered exactly when I had begun to disappoint her so much. I supposed I was too busy being happy and enjoying my life. Frolicking around with Glyn and dreaming of a simple life.

"I'm hungry, Aggie." I couldn't wait any longer as we led the horses down Savory Lane.

"We can stop. What are you in the mood for?" I was shocked. I thought she was still punishing me. My mouth began to water.

"Everything!" I shouted, digging a handful of copper urchins and silver mollusks from my gatherings bag. We stopped at four different vendors and carried a basket filled with warm bread, salty baked potatoes, a pile of roasted vegetables, and two fat, sticky cinnamon buns back to the wagon. I ripped into the bread while we walked, glad that my mouth was too full to talk. And I finally allowed myself to think of Glyn. I started to concoct a plan. I would go see him while Aggie napped. She was going to need a nap before we went back to the forest for the Ghostmoth Hex at midnight.

Aggie summoned her illumins around the little folding table and set out two plates, the napkins I embroidered for her sixtieth birthday, and the silverware I had polished once a week since I could hold a fork. I sent the horses to the pasture and let the little bantams out to peck at the ground for grubs.

"Jesobel, do you remember the Viperberry Hex?" she asked when I plopped down on a painted stool to eat.

"I think so," I said, not caring whether I did or didn't. I was too busy wolfing down my food.

"You think so? Or you do?" snapped Aggie.

"I do, Aggie. I do." Her attitude was making me nervy and all wound up. I just wanted to relax and eat in peace!

"Say it. Say the hex," she demanded between dainty old-lady bites.

I repeated the words, messing them up about three-quarters through, and caught myself too late. Damn it.

"Again," she smacked her fork down on the table, rattling the plates and glasses. I would have given a million golden pearls for a soothing mug of licorice beer right then. It took me five more tries to finally get it right, and I was worried that Aggie had gotten herself so worked up that she might make herself ill.

"Now the Bleakhound Hex. Go."

I got this one right on the first try, to my great relief, and to Aggie's utter astonishment. Complete shock, really.

"Fine. We better get some sleep before we go back. It's been a long day."

"You can say that again," I mumbled, closing my eyes with a sigh. But sleep was not on my agenda.

I cleared the table, hoping Aggie would go to bed while I cleaned the dishes, but she kept to her declaration and didn't let me out of her sight. When the dishes were washed and dried and put back in the corner cupboard, I undressed to my bloomers and camisole and crawled into my berth. Despite my plans to sneak out to see Glyn, I was asleep before Aggie started snoring, the music from the Quickfire drifting through the windows like a lullaby on the wind.

CHAPTER 17

I opened my eyes with a start when I felt a soft tapping below my berth. Glyn! Finally! A mixture of relief, excitement, and a hint of terror washed over me, stirring my insides.

I crawled out of bed, glad I hadn't closed my berth doors, and pulled on my skirt and bodice, yanking at the laces. By the time I crept to the door, Glyn had already opened it a sliver and his face was silhouetted against the moonlit sky.

"Hey," I whispered, slipping through the crack. "What are you doing here?"

"I've been looking for you all day," he grinned, his sea-green eyes annoyingly attractive.

"I'm sorry. I've been wanting to talk to you. Aggie has kept me on a short leash. I'm sorry about the other day," I said.

"It's okay, Jessa. I know you've got a lot on your mind. Wanna go shoot some arrows?"

"Sure!" I said, glad he didn't suggest kissing or talking about what would happen to us once I was gone, despite that being all I'd been thinking about for days. I grabbed my bow and arrows, pulled on my cloak and followed Glyn. His lanky step had such a confident swagger to it; not cocky—just that sort of self-assuredness that made you want to be near him. I sighed when I thought of how confused I was about us. And I balled my fist when I thought of that redhead. Which made me want to kiss him just to spite her. Which was so wrong. *Grrr!*

Lost in my thoughts, I didn't even notice when Glyn headed east down the hill, away from the range and toward the herd grazing near the bathing spring.

"On horseback?" said Glyn with a huge grin, and I saw his muscles twitch ever so slightly, and knew he was going to run.

"You'll never beat me on horseback, Glyn Carter!" I took off, and he was right there with me. He passed with his lengthy stride, but I whistled low and pushed myself faster. It felt good to run. The wind smelled like starlight and the air tasted just as sparkly and with a hint of sea salt. It was cool, but not too cold, and I was free, racing across the grass after Glyn, my toes thrilled to be out of my boots. It almost seemed like we were kids again, like my lonely, horrible, magical future was not just a day away. Like the night would last forever and ever.

"I'm gonna whoop you!" I yelled, laughing and reaching forward mid-stride to smack him on the hip. His legs were longer than mine, and I knew he was going just fast enough to make me believe he was really trying to beat me, but we both knew he was about to kick it into high gear and leave me in the dust. Firefly heard me on the third whistle and trotted across the field to pick me up. I was on his back just as Glyn reached his horse, and I spun Firefly around and raced up the hill past the market, past the arenas and all the way around the lake to the archery range with Glyn and Django eating our dust.

We galloped through the range, letting arrows fly into the targets as fast as we could. When my quiver was empty Firefly tucked around and skidded to a stop.

"How many did you hit?" Glyn grinned, skidding up beside us. He had been trying to beat me for the past two years, and failing every time.

"I hit them all, duh." I said, with a little too much sass.

"I'll be the judge of that." Glyn clucked at his gelding and they skipped off, and we were right by his side. He leaned over to yank one of my arrows out of a target.

"Oh, look at that, bullseye. Oh, bullseye again. What's this? Another bullseye? Typical!" He waved my third arrow at me with a sarcastic smile.

"It's not easy being this good," I said, shrugging nonchalantly. "But I hear you've been practicing." I smirked, leaning out to collect the rest of my arrows. "Oh! Look at this! Did I get a bullseye? And what's this? Another bullseye. Oh, and another, and another! And what about this one? Bullseye again. How many did you say you got so far?"

"Fine, you win again," he said, yanking the rest of his arrows from their targets. He was kind enough not to point out that all of his shots were bullseyes, too. But I noticed.

"You *have* been practicing, I see. Impressive."

Glyn spun his horse around. "Wanna go again?"

But I didn't. I just wanted to ride a little. "Not really. I already beat you once. I'd hate to beat you again," I teased, knowing full well it was a tie, fair and square. "How about a ride?"

Glyn laughed, that easy, deep laugh that resonated in my bones. "To Bat Rock?"

"Sure."

We followed the sea wall that runs along the cliff west toward Saggita and came across the huge rock that juts out in a most precarious way over the sea—a dizzying distance below.

Glyn slid down off Django and lifted me down from Firefly. Unnecessary, but sweet. He took my hand, and our fingers stitched seamlessly together. Glyn's palm felt warm and familiar, and a rush of heat surprised me, along with an increasing desire to kiss him, followed by a remembered flash of copper hair and a sharp twinge of jealousy. We clambered out to the rock, Glyn never letting go of my hand until we were seated, and even then, he only let go to put his arm around me and pull me into him. I leaned my head on his shoulder and watched the reflections of the moons on the dark water so far below. We'd sat like this countless times, but this time, every place where my body touched his was electric and confusing.

"I wonder if we'll ever see that big white bat again?" he asked.

"I hope not. It might carry Firefly or Django off into the night. That thing was gigantic!"

"I know. It was freakishly huge," agreed Glyn, and there was a quiet pause, in which we were both remembering the way Glyn screamed like a girl when it flapped out from below us like a living ship's sail and skimmed our heads as it winged haphazardly into the night, and for the first time, we didn't both erupt in laughter. Instead, I snuggled into his shoulder, feeling suddenly about to weep. It hadn't hit me until right that second just how much I would miss Glyn.

"So, I've been thinking," said Glyn.

"You know I hate it when you do that." I blinked a sneaky tear away and pressed myself closer to him.

"We can do this, Jessa."

I sat silent, a million thoughts rushing through my head, a trillion feelings tumbling inside my chest. Aggie's warning, the centuries-old tradition, Seraphina. How deeply I loved this boy and what would really be the right thing to do.

"We can't." I said, surprised at my answer.

Truth was, I wished so hard we could. I sniffed his neck. His blond hair tickled my nose. Before I even realized what I was doing, I moved his hair aside and softly kissed him just below his ear. There was an awkward pause as Glyn tried to register what I had said. I was equally stunned, and suddenly wanted to jump off the cliff and fly away on that giant bat.

"Yes we can, Jessa. You know we can." He kissed the top of my head. It was warm and comforting and it made me want to cry.

"Glyn, everything just got ten times more complicated than it was. Maybe a hundred times worse."

"What could be more complicated than you leaving for a year, and then only being able to see you a few moons at a time?" He grinned at me, his hand on my cheek, his eyes an endless sea of green, and squeezed my hand, so confident in his love for me, so confident that we could make this sorry arrangement work.

I smiled sadly at him, and squeezed his hand back, and looked away at the horizon, off into the salty abyss below.

"I have to tell you something. Something terrible." A gust of wind blew sideways, blowing my unruly hair into Glyn's face.

"What? What is it?" He smoothed my hair and took my face in his hands, his eyes searching mine for a clue.

"Look," I said, pulling my blouse down to reveal the invisible compass above my heart, the weight of it heavier than anything I'd ever felt.

"I don't see anything, Jessa. What's the matter?"

"It's the Legend of Azimuth, Glyn. It's true. It's me. There is a compass on my chest. Apparently it's been there since I was a baby. I'm not sure what activates it, but it's there. And you know what that means…"

"Whew, is that all? I thought you were going to say something crazy about us not being able to make this work." He laughed. But my stomach tumbled and tightened. I felt sick. That's exactly what I was about to say.

"It's not funny, Glyn. I'm serious. Do you even remember the Legend?"

"Of course I do. Blah blah LEGEND blah blah. So what?"

"So what? So when I was simply learning to be a Magic Weaver, that was one thing. I can even stand the idea of being Starkeeper, sort of. I can even handle the part in the legend about leading us all back to

Pyxis. What I can't handle is that bit about the epic war. You know, the war that the Heart of Azimuth is supposed to start. The fate of the entire world is in my hands, Glyn!"

Glyn wrapped his arms around me, pulled me close and said nothing. "We'll figure this out, Jessa. We'll figure it out together. Don't worry." It felt so good in his arms, I almost believed him. But there was a darkness that churned just below that compass. Something dangerous and terrifying clawing at the insides of my heart, my quickflame.

Something told me to let Glyn go. That it was the only thing to do. It wouldn't be fair to drag him into all of this. I put my lips against his neck, inhaling the clean scent of clove soap, and planted another small kiss there.

"I have to get back," I said. "Aggie will be looking for me soon. We have to go back into the woods tonight. I have to learn one last hex." But my lips tingled with the warmth left there by the smooth skin of Glyn's neck, and a confusing flutter erupted in my stomach. I backed myself up as Glyn leaned toward me, and lowered myself off the rock, barely dodging his attempt at a real kiss, and cursing myself for not taking advantage of it. But Aggie's words rang out in my head for the millionth time.

He loves you, Jessa. You know that. Love can overcome darn near every obstacle. But you think long and hard before you break that boy's heart.

Trouble is, I was going to break his heart either way, and I knew it. I just needed to figure out which way I could live with. If I could live with either way at all.

CHAPTER 18

I'd barely crawled into my berth and was asleep for what felt like five seconds when Aggie scraped the doors noisily aside. It was pitch black.

"Get up!" she said.

I smelled tea and I was grateful. I was going to need it. My stomach churned with delirious tiredness.

Aggie lit a lamp and tinkered around in the cupboard where she stored all of her herbs and powders and vials and jars of things she used for charms and spells while I stumbled to the table and plopped down to drink my tea, rubbing my puffy, sleep-deprived eyes.

"The ghostmoths are dangerous, Jesobel. They are pure Mystic magic. A thousand times more powerful than any Orphic hex could ever wish to be."

"Mmmhmmm," I mumbled through a gulp of coffee. "Hot! Ow! Tongue! Burning!" I frowned at Aggie and stuck out my tongue to cool it, feeling sorry for myself. This was going to be one of those days. Or middle-of-the-nights. Whatever. I felt a disaster coming on.

"Jesobel!" Aggie smacked her hand down on the table and leaned into me with a steely glare. "You must focus! Honestly, I don't know what's come over you these past few months."

I wanted to shout at her, tell her that I didn't CARE about magic, that I didn't WANT to learn magic, that I didn't ASK to be the Starkeeper, and that I probably wasn't the right person for the job anyway. That this whole compass thing was freaking me out and that I had left Glyn crushed that I had made up my mind about him, and now I was having second thoughts. But that look she gave me, well, it could kill a person, and for some reason I wasn't quite ready to die. Even though the disappointment in her eyes sort of made me shrivel up and wish I was dead. I just sat there.

"I'm thorry, Aggie," I lisped, pulling my scorched tongue back into my mouth. I stared into my tea cup, willing it to cool, and tried to become invisible.

"Sorry doesn't cut it, Jessa. Listen, I know you think it's unfair that your life is about to change, and that the life you imagine for yourself will never be. I have done my best to train you well. I have spent every day of your life preparing you for your duties and your destiny. I have always had faith in you. I have always believed that at some point, you would stop daydreaming and focus on the life that lies before you. But your attitude is even starting to make *me* wonder if you're cut out for this." She spun on her heel and started cramming things into a bag, her curls buzzing with fury.

"But, Aggie, nobody even *uses* magic anymore. And it's banished here! Why do I have to learn magic? It just seems so… pointless." I regretted the words the second they left my lips, and I wished I could take back the whiny sound of them.

Aggie's curls stopped quaking, and she went deathly still, a stony statue with one hand still wrapped around something shoved deep in her gatherings bag. The stillness filled the room, sucked the oxygen from it, and I could scarcely breathe. She was going to scream at me, I knew it. I slunk down into my seat and cowered, waiting for her to turn around and unleash her fury at me.

Instead, she eventually took a deep breath, dropped whatever it was into the bag, and straightened her slender shoulders. She slowly turned to me, and said nothing, just scanned my face searching for something she clearly didn't see, based on the way she sighed a little and flicked her eyes as if she'd finally accepted the truth about me. There was an ache that radiated from the middle of my chest—it got stuck in the back of my throat and I couldn't tell if I wanted to cry or throw up.

"I didn't mean it," I whispered. But the whisper was a lie. She knew it. I knew it. I was just the wrong girl for this job. I couldn't help it! I had a lot on my mind. Glyn for one thing… to marry, or not to marry… I had made up my mind, but it was killing me! Why did he have to kiss me in the first place? Everything was perfect the way it was when I pretended we were just friends. That kiss ruined everything! Or was is Seraphina's kiss that ruined everything? Was I just jealous?! I didn't even know anymore!

Aggie shook her head at me in that sad, pathetic way that made me feel like I'd just murdered puppies, and without warning I was so mad I felt like I *could* murder a puppy. The wagon suddenly closed in on me like a prison. I pushed past Aggie and stomped down the stairs into the dark night, unsure of what to do with the snarl of hot anger and suffocating sadness knotting up like mystic eels in my stomach, my throat. I wanted to scream. Instead I shoved my feet in my pretty new boots and whistled for Firefly. I heard him whinny from across the field, and this made me more angry. I stomped behind our shoppe, wanting to smash dishes against the wagon just to hear the satisfying shatter and to see all of the fragments go flying.

Firefly must have sensed my need for a mood change—he trotted up and shoved me with the bridge of his nose. He knew exactly how hard to push me so that I stumbled but didn't fall. When I gained my balance, he shoved me again. And again. But this time, I didn't erupt in laughter, I got madder. I pushed him back and stomped to the back of the wagon to sulk. I sat on the bantam cage and listened to their soft clucks and purrs. In three seconds my face was soaked with tears and the rage inside of me solidified into some sort of heavy thing. A heavy thing that had burrowed into my heart and planned to stay there forever. I took a deep breath, the anger moved aside just a little, and a weighty melancholy took root.

After a few minutes, Firefly strutted around the corner with Aggie on his back, Pennyfeathers trailing behind. I wiped my eyes across the back of my sleeve and stood up, trying to act normal.

For the first time, I saw Aggie as someone other than that sweet old lady that was like a mother to me. She looked ferocious, electric, surrounded by her green spark fairies. Astride Firefly, she was some supernatural force to be reckoned with, something not of this world, something purely of the Mystic.

For the first time, I realized how much power and magic lived within her quickflame, how direct her access was to the Mystic, and it was as if a rug had been pulled out from under me. Everything went sliding sideways briefly, blurring and shifting, and nothing looked the same when the world came back into focus. I felt small and stupid, but I couldn't understand why.

"Come," said Aggie. And I hopped on Penny and followed behind her without a word.

Aggie rode bridleless, though Firefly had a colorful embroidered pad decorated with tiny mirrors and edged with tassels belted to his girth. Aggie was fast and focused, and something about how tiny she was compared to how seriously gigantic she seemed was unsettling in a way I couldn't explain.

CHAPTER 19

When we reached the woods, I felt as if I'd been riding behind Aggie and Firefly in a wake of powerful magic. My entire body tingled with it, and it was eerie and unnerving. Aggie motioned for me to dismount, and then whispered to Firefly and Pennyfeathers to stay hidden, but to not follow us. I stepped under the canopy with heightened senses, disliking the fact we left the horses and anxious over the memories of the bleakhounds.

Aggie crept along the forest floor without making a sound, and I did my best to mimic her, though where I stepped, twigs snapped and leaves crunched, sending nightingales and whip-poor-wills warbling and flittering through dark leaves. The moons were full and cast a blue glow above the treetops that only reached through the canopy wherever a bare hole was left by a fallen tree. Here and there, shimmery swaths of pale moonlight filtered into the darkness, eerily lighting our way.

I followed Aggie as she threaded between the budding branches in some mysterious pattern. At first I thought she'd lost her mind as she traveled between certain trees, around them, and looped back on our path like a crazy person. Her inefficient way of getting from point A to point B consumed me with frustration, but I shut my mouth and followed her because she seemed really, really serious.

After a while, my body noticed familiar motions and it was clear that she was drawing something, a huge pattern or symbol amidst the trees, over and over and over with our bodies mapping the way. I wondered what it would look like from above, if our dance with the trees were visible—some sort of mandala or sigil? I didn't have to wait long to find out.

The ghostmoths appeared, releasing the bright, tart scent of quickbane blossoms, which tickled my nose in comparison to the thick loamy aroma of the forest floor.

The whole moth thing was not what I expected. I don't know what I expected, but this was not it. First, the Mystic dust began to sparkle out behind us, and the symbol weaved through the trees, alight with Mystic magic—pure quickflame. The magic was soft, soothing, yet the power of it was undeniably and immensely strong. It was the sort of power that begins in your belly and radiates out to all parts of your body, so that even the tips of your hair feel tingly. It made me a little bit giddy.

When we closed the final loop on the symbol, which was huge and spanned a gigantic section of the forest, Aggie put a hand up, and I stopped in my tracks. I gazed at the shimmering trail behind me, and saw that the Mystic dust was alive. It floated like motes, but it was luminous and moving in a way that regular dust didn't. I wanted to touch it, but Aggie smacked my hand away.

"Be still," she warned, and her voice was grave. Meanwhile, I wanted to giggle. The Mystic dust was playful and tickly, even if it wasn't touching me directly. It was fizzy and bubbly and it made my nose itch, like licorice beer, even though it was just swirling in the air. Its beauty mystified me, and I had an urge to blow on it, to watch it dance, but Aggie's iron gaze warned me to control myself.

I was scorched with jealousy when Aggie took a breath and blew into the dust, sending a ripple of wild energy curling through the particles. It changed color as her breath sped around the symbol, all the way through the forest, in and out and around and around so many tree trunks until it returned to Aggie and the symbol had been activated. It vibrated, shimmering in shades of blues and purples. I realized suddenly that we were standing in a small circle at its center, and that we had, indeed, drawn some sort of enormous sigil, which now levitated at eye level above the forest floor.

There was a small clearing where we stood—there were no trees within our little circle—and from it the big moon, Alcyone, could be seen directly above, smiling sadly down on us with her wan light. She always made me feel as if she were lonely, endlessly searching the skies for her lost love, the second sun, with their six little children trailing behind her. Poor Alcyone would never find her sun husband, who now jettisoned through space splintered into so many cold bits of rock and ice. I wondered what Vale was like when there were two suns?

In front of my nose, the first ghostmoth blinked into existence hovering near the sparkling dust ring. I couldn't seem to fight my urge to blow on the shimmering fragments very well. I hadn't tried it yet, because Aggie looked ready to maim me if I did, but I wanted to so bad it was becoming comical. To me, anyway. I suppressed a giggle.

"Look, Aggie!" I whispered, pointing my finger at it, so close. I wanted to touch it.

Aggie sucked in a breath, "Jesobel. Don't move." Her voice shook with fear. I didn't see what the big deal was; it had a cute fuzzy face and inquisitive black eyes.

The moth was extraordinary to look at. Its tiny eyes seemed to peer into my soul. It moved like a hummingbird, hovering there, as if waiting for me to turn into a moonblossom or something, ready to sip my nectar. The wings were glasslike, veined with swirling shapes and sections like itty-bitty leaded glass windows edged in velvet, and its downy flowing tail looped and curled in a way that was elegant and lovely. I was mesmerized by its beauty, and the way it shifted in and out of the Mystic so that I was confused as to whether it was even real. It was there and gone and back again in a flash. I lifted my hand to allow it to perch on my finger, and Aggie tackled me to the ground.

"Haven't you heard anything I've told you all these years, Jesobel!"

The venom in her voice reduced me to a naughty child. Now that she mentioned it, I did recall about a thousand ghostmoth stories. *Never, never, never touch them.* That was the rule. Oh yeah. Ooops.

Aggie left me in a heap on the ground feeling ashamed of myself and did something to fix whatever hole I just ripped in the Mystic sigil. She shot me dirty looks every chance she got, and I realized I better put some effort into paying attention.

I stood up and straightened my skirts, smoothed my bodice and tried to look studious, wishing there was a tree in our magic circle that I could lean on. I hid my sleepy yawns whenever she turned her back on me.

The ghostmoths came, many at a time, and I realized that they were bound to the Mystic dust. They couldn't leave it, and so they flitted in its path like fish in a river, more and more and more of them flickering in and out of existence every second. Aggie blew on the dust again, and the ripples went out, directing the path of the ghostmoths, their glassine wings throwing strange reflections in the purpling sparkles, their velvety bodies soft as rabbit fur, and feathery antennae twitching this way and that.

Aggie checked the moon. Alcyone was almost exactly in the middle of our circle in the center of the glowing symbol.

She waited for something invisible to happen, and when it did—I had no idea what it was—Aggie lifted a small glass bottle and touched the dust with the opening. She recited some words—I had no clue what they meant—and the first ghostmoth to complete the path of our symbol was sucked into the bottle with a puff of Mystic dust.

I didn't know how it fit in there, because the moth was easily as big as two of my hands, and the bottle was so teensy its fuzzy head shouldn't even fit inside it. Aggie mumbled some words, and the ghostmoths vanished in tiny bursts all around the forest on our Mystic dust trail, until all that was left was ordinary dust, falling heavily and un-magically to the ground to disappear among the moon-bathed leaves.

Aggie put a cork on the bottle, trapping the ghostmoth inside. The bottle had a chain attached to it, and she looped it over my head. She drew a picture in front of my heart, where the ghostmoth hung, and touched her finger to the bottle, pushing it into my chest.

Quickflame, hot and searing, made a bright circle there. I screamed, my hand flying to the trail left by the burning light, and looked down at my chest. My eyes traced the circle, the arrows, the intricate patterns that raced across my skin. I sucked in a breath. The compass! Lighting me up like a beacon in the dark forest! I stumbled backward and looked at Aggie, betrayal blazing in my heart. It was true! Myriam *had* seen it! Aggie had lied to me my entire life!

A blast of hot quickflame entered my body as the light show on my chest completed its rounds, and a river of my spark fairies blasted out of the way and clung to my hair, frightened. I put my hand over the compass, its violet light cutting blades into the darkness, escaping from between my fingers. I eyed Aggie with a furious glare.

"Why didn't you tell me," I spat. "Why? The legend is true! And it's just a matter of time before horrible things begin to happen. Why didn't you tell me, Aggie?!"

Aggie ignored me. She gathered her things and began walking out the way we came, untwisting around the trees, un-looping and un-zigzagging all over the place, unraveling whatever sigil the dance produced on the way in.

"Aggie, why didn't you tell me?" I shouted at her again. She didn't blink an eye. When we reached the horses, they were serene, and the hills below were quiet all the way to the gate. The market was still, the Quickfire burning low, and still Aggie wouldn't say a word about the trapped ghostmoth hanging around my neck or the itchy glowing compass slowly fading from my chest.

I didn't understand why she was ignoring me. I fumed with every step. Wasn't it enough that I had to be the Starkeeper when I didn't even want to? And the Keeper of the stupid Secret? Now, I was the Heart of Azimuth, too? The damned Way-Bringer? As if people didn't despise me enough! My existence would soon bring about a devastating prophecy whose ending was unwritten, but it didn't look promising, not with me in charge of writing it! Would have been nice to know that the fate of the world was in my hands. It would have been nice to be able to actually prepare for this!

I clenched my teeth and followed Aggie in silence, repeating the legend over in my mind, looking for some clue that this compass on my chest was just a freakish coincidence, so that I didn't have to hate the woman who had raised me for keeping me clueless to my fate. To the fate of the world.

I had always known that when I turned sixteen, my life would never be the same. But I didn't see this coming, and the more I thought about it, the more I felt like shouting at Aggie. She should have been preparing me for *this*, not for becoming Starkeeper! Who cared about the stupid Starkeeper when the entire world would eventually be in the biggest Mystic battle in the history of the Eighty-Eight Realms of Vale?

When we passed down Tinker's Lane on our way to Mystic Alley, I wished I could throw pebbles at Glyn's window and take one final ride back to Bat Rock, back to Glyn's safe arms.

Aggie put her things away silently and when I lifted the ghostmoth chain from my neck, Aggie warned, "No. Never take it off, Jesobel. Not without a damned good reason."

Even though my mind whirled with unanswered questions, and I didn't understand what being the Heart of Azimuth really meant in relation to being the next Royal Starkeeper, Aggie wasn't talking, except to say, "You better finish that drawing of Firefly."

It was now or never, and suddenly, throwing myself into the role of Starkeeper-to-Be was the only thing that made sense to do, since it was the only thing I had any training for at all.

I wanted to scream at her, ask her about the compass, about the legend, ask her what I was supposed to do, when this war was supposed to begin. But she didn't seem even the slightest bit willing to hear me. So I crawled into my berth for the last time and scribbled my horse angrily with a stump of pencil, and waited for her to go to sleep. I needed to talk to Glyn, not about that kiss, or that nasty redhead, but about everything else.

CHAPTER 20

Sixteen only felt different than fifteen because it was the day I was to depart for Corona Australis for my coronation. I wasn't sure if every Starkeeper from all of the Eighty-Eight Realms would be present, but I tried not to think about it, or else I would be sick. I wasn't allowed to bring Firefly with me, and I couldn't bear the thought of parting with him, even for a year. I had been lying to myself that they might make an exception and allow him on the ship. At least I'd still have him on the month-long journey to the harbor.

"Good Morning, Aggie," I shouted, returning from an early walk down the quiet, sleeping marketplace lanes.

"Happy Birthday, my dear Jessa," she boomed, all confusing smiles and happiness. "Sixteen. My goodness how time flies."

She touched my cheek briefly and a sad mist danced across her eyes. Maybe it was the hexes that had been upsetting her so much. Or maybe she just finally got a good night's sleep, but she was being so nice that I didn't know what to make of her. It was as if the last grueling year of her punishing looks never existed; as if that whole bleakhound and ghostmoth insanity had never happened; as if there wasn't a living compass etched into my flesh. A relieving sense of home enveloped me.

"Have you had your breakfast, dear? Today's the day!" She squeezed my hand so tightly that I knew this was her way of starting our goodbye. I savored the feeling of her nimble old fingers woven between mine, her soft skin sliding over brittle bones, and did my best to keep from crying. It was such a relief to see her smile finally, but it made the idea of moving into my own wagon come into sharp, painful focus. It was harder to think about leaving when she wasn't being so mean to me.

"I have, and I'm all ready to go see Uncle Fin and Aunt Myriam. I stayed up all night trying to draw Firefly just right. I think I finally got him, see?" I couldn't bear the thought of leaving Aggie's wagon later tonight. I needed to pretend it was any other birthday. Any other Quickbane Festival. I shoved the drawing in Aggie's face.

"Not so close, Jessa. I may be a bit deaf, but I can see just fine." She pushed the parchment away from her nose. "Yes, yes, I think you've got it. He looks nothing like a spotted sausage now. You even got that star on his forehead just right. Oh! And these vines are a perfect touch. You'll have to tell me all about this as we walk. Where's our fuzzy birthday boy? I have some carrots for him."

I whistled. The low, long whistle rose slightly in pitch, and by the time it was done, Firefly waltzed around the corner with a twinkle in his eye, ready for anything.

"Over here, Firefly. Aggie needs a ride."

He stepped his giant, hairy hooves carefully through the camp, mindful to avoid pots and pans hanging over the fire pit, and navigated deftly around the bantam cage, noisy with clucky hens, and then stepped over some basket-weaving supplies near the curved stair where Aggie perched, waiting with carrots.

"Happy Birthday, you Mystical beast. You take care of Jessa, now, and bring her back to us safe and sound next year. Got that?" She scruffed his forelock. He mowed through the carrots during her not-so-secret message and then crept toward the stair still crunching the last one. It took me a minute to realize what she had just said.

"Aggie! Does this mean he can come with me?" She winked with a wide grin, and I enveloped her in a tenacious hug. "How did you do it!" My heart swelled to bursting with happiness.

"I have my ways." The old woman wrestled free from my embrace and climbed aboard my stallion's wide back with a little help from me, and we were off, marching through the marketplace on a fine spring day, the final day of the Quickbane Festival. My sixteenth birthday. The day without time. The day that would change everything, forever. I was to set out alone in my new wagon at moonrise. I would follow the caravan as far as the Seven Bridges Road, and then follow Fin to Wither's Way and then drive on to Saggita where Firefly would... *not!*... stay with Fin, and we would board the Queen's ship to Corona Australis. In a month's time, we would be setting foot and hoof upon the great City of Ice to swap spells with my great-grandmother before she passed her crown to me at the Royal Coronation.

I couldn't help it. Even with Firefly at my side, I despised the thought of leaving. I sighed, heavy-hearted, as uncle Fin's wagon came into view, parked alongside mine, which was still completely hidden beneath a mass of sailcloth. For one brief second, I felt like running far away, and never coming back. But then I realized that my year of hard work and worry about drawing designs for my very own Starkeeper-worthy wagon home was about to come to an end. That, at least, was another small relief.

Fin had worked so hard to make it beautiful for me, I knew. He'd been away in Sugar Hollow building it and painting it for nearly eight months, and was so excited to show me what he'd done. Myriam had been working on the interior. Aside from being a skilled seamstress, she did all the gilding with paper-thin sheets of gold leaf for Fin's wagons. And mine would have ridiculous amounts of it. I had never seen Starkeeper Yarrow's sailboat—she was a seafaring Pyxie—but I had heard about how it glittered in the sun, and how a pod of dolphins escorted her everywhere she went.

I knew that Fin had kept the spot above the door blank for my final rendering of Firefly and would finish it before the fairyworks went off, and knowing him, he would make me wait until then to see the entire wagon.

I exhaled a bigger sigh, this one a determined, fate-accepting sort of sigh, but there was no hiding the fact that I was tense and scared to death. I knew my wagon would be beautiful, and I would learn to love it and I would learn to love my life—at least until I potentially started this legendary magical war Aggie wouldn't tell me anything else about. (I hoped that her silence just meant that it wasn't an immediate threat, and that Starkeeper Yarrow would prepare me for that fate.) I just couldn't believe this day was actually here, and my last night in Aggie's wagon was already behind me.

After handing my drawing over to Fin, Aggie escorted me to Myriam's tent. She gave me the rest of my birthday to spend at the marketplace and to visit with Glyn, provided I cleaned myself up and didn't leave Myriam's shoppe until I looked like a proper Starkeeper-in-Waiting.

"Let me see you," Aggie said, buckling my corset tight and standing back to admire me.

The new lacy petticoats itched my legs and I hated the stiff, bright purple skirt. I wanted to wear my comfy leather corset and my soft, airy cotton skirts. I tried to smile at Aunt Myriam, who had made the new clothes for me in a style that mixed the latest Orion hemlines with our traditional, long Pyxie hem for an asymmetrical look that made no sense to me. She had been dying to dress me up in fancy clothes for the past year. I felt awkward at best.

"The violet matches your eyes, Jesobel. You look beautiful!" Myriam squealed, clipping a sparkly barrette into my hair to hold up the ribbons and braids that she had worked into some fancy configuration I would never be able to repeat on my own.

I fidgeted and wanted to scratch and pull everything off, and let my hair down. I was horribly embarrassed to let Glyn see me like this.

Myriam rubbed a shimmery powder onto my eyelids, another one on my cheeks, and combed kohl through my eyelashes with a tiny metal brush. She shoved me toward a tall looking-glass and handed me a small pot of pinkish balm. "Use your finger and dab this on your lips," she instructed. I squirmed, eager to leave.

"Do I have to?" I didn't recognize the girl reflected back at me. "Ew! No! I won't do it. I look so... so..." I turned a little to see the pile of ribbons woven into my hair. "I'm so... purple!" I turned my back to the glass and tears stung the corners of my eyes.

"Jesobel, don't be ridiculous! You are absolutely stunning. Come here." Myriam mauled my face with a glob of balm on her finger and smeared it on my mouth. "Stand still or it will be all over your face."

"I'm just going to wipe it off," I pouted.

"If you wipe it on that silk sleeve, I will personally hire Aggie to hex you to the moons and back!"

"Fine. I won't. I'm sorry, Myriam. I just don't feel like myself in all these fancy girly things."

Aggie's face grew stern and cold. "But you're about to become our Starkeeper, Jesobel. You need to start looking the part," she said curtly. "And you *must* start behaving like a Royal."

Myriam grinned and tucked a stray curl back with a hairpin and spun me around to face the mirror again. "Just look. You are so lovely!"

I glanced at the silver glass to satisfy them and pretended to agree, though I was horrified by how my eyelashes looked two leagues too long and my lips were far too pink and shiny. And what was that silly fairy dust on my cheeks and eyelids? I wanted to drag the back of my fist across my face and erase all of it. Never mind that my clothes looked like some sort of insane decoration that belonged on top of a fancy cake.

"Can I go now? Please? I have barely talked to Glyn since autumn!"

"Well he won't be able to resist you looking like that!" Myriam giggled and Aggie pursed her lips.

"Stay off that horse in those skirts, young lady! And absolutely no archery today."

"Fiiiiiine," I growled, grabbing my gatherings bag, into which I had already emptied the contents of my old skirt pockets.

"Ah-ah-ah," tsked Myriam. "I made you a pretty purse to match."

I sighed, defeated. There was no way I was going to win this one. I took the lace-ruffled thing and dumped the contents of my leather gatherings bag into it, guiltily noticing the nyxiegram I never opened, and watched in horror as the amulet dropped to the ground.

"What's this?" asked Myriam, picking up the amulet.

"Oh, I found it near the archery range. Do you recognize it?" I didn't want to get into that whole story right then, and I didn't want Aggie asking questions about it. Especially after graduating to Magic Weaver. She was so proud of me. I didn't want to risk ruining that.

"I've never seen anything like it. It's unusual. Quite pretty. Lucky find! Here, I'll pin it to your purse." Myriam looped the purse over my head and slid it to my hip, securing the amulet near the base of the strap. I shifted it out of Aggie's view. "And you'll need this," she said, handing me a dainty coin pouch.

I dug the loose copper urchins and silver limpets from the bottom of the purse and shoved them into the coin pouch, snapping it shut and cramming it into the frilly new bag as fast as I could.

"Okay," I said, hiding the amulet beneath my hand. "*Now* may I go?" It was such a perfect spring day outside, I didn't want to waste another second of it with this nonsense. My desire to spend a final day with Glyn was nearing an agonizing level, made even more excruciating by the fact that I would have to face him in this ridiculous, humiliating outfit.

Myriam looked at my bare feet and made a sad, clucking noise.

"You almost forgot your new boots!"

"What new boots?" I sighed, but I wanted to scream. Myriam giggled and ran into a dressing tent. She returned dangling a pair of the most incredible boots I had ever seen.

"I had these made special for you, Jessa. I know how you like to be barefoot. Look, you can even wear your bells with them!"

The boots could hardly be called boots. They had cutouts all over that allowed my toes to be free, my calves to breathe, and were tooled with just the right amount of curlicues. They were the softest leather and I was actually excited to try them on. I tackled Myriam in a bear hug.

"I love them! Thank you, Myriam."

"Be back by supper time, please, Jesobel. It's graduation day," snapped Aggie.

"Thank you!" I tried not to run out of Myriam's huge shoppe tent, which was packed with scores of fancy gowns for the Quickbane Ball. The wealthiest brightborns would be visiting all day to retrieve their custom orders placed the year prior. Myriam was practically famous for her immaculate designs.

I walked as elegantly as a girl in new boots being strangled by itchy clothes could manage until the tent was far enough behind me, and then I ran to the end of the lane, hoping nobody was looking at me. The only parts of my entire self that felt remotely familiar were the tiny bells on my ankles and my nearly bare feet. I relished the feel of soft dandelions brushing past my toes, but my new clothes itched and scratched all over.

As soon as I was around the corner, I whistled for Firefly while fighting an urge to tear all of the barrettes and hairpins from my braids.

His heavy hooves thundered down the lane, and I marveled at the way his feathered feet swept the grass like soft dust brooms as he came toward me.

He skidded around and whinnied, happy to see me. Or maybe he was laughing at me, I couldn't tell. "Shhh," I scolded. "I'm not supposed to ride today." I climbed onto his back and turned him away from Myriam's tent. "Let's go find Glyn!"

I headed toward the archery range, wishing I had my quiver and bow. When we crested the hill at a full gallop, I was surprised to see the range was deserted aside from one of Starkeeper Rowan's armored watchmen wandering through the course on his tall sport horse, looking down as if he'd lost an arrow. I immediately urged Firefly to turn around, not in the mood to be harassed.

"You there!" he shouted, my stocky horse unable to turn away quickly enough.

I ignored the watchman's call and clucked Firefly into a run straight back down the hill.

"Get back here, Pyxie! By order of Starkeeper Rowan!"

I thought about pretending I didn't hear him, and then thought better of it. I slowed Firefly just as the watchman skidded up next to us on his hot-tempered horse, nearly taking my leg off in the process. I wanted to shout at him for being so daft, but instead, I had Firefly step sideways away from the man, and halt, facing him.

The watchman lifted his helmet and scanned me head to toe with a look in his eye that made me feel ill. My leg felt suddenly too bare where the fancy hemline crept up and up above my knee. Even my toes felt too nude in my new boots. Firefly backed up a few steps, taut with energy and ready to bolt.

"What?" I asked, knowing I was probably not speaking correctly or politely to the Starkeeper's watchman.

"Well, aren't you a pretty little Pyxie wench?" He edged his horse closer, his eyes slithering up and down my leg.

My cheeks grew hot, matching a bitter heat that brewed in my stomach. A heat that longed for my bow and quiver.

"What do you want?" I asked again. If he looked at me like that for one more second, I would take off without asking permission. Which was against the Starkeeper's rules. With that stupid notice nailed to every pole and tree in sight, I figured running might give him reason to accuse me of doing magic. As much as I wasn't looking forward to my future, I knew I didn't want to spend it locked up in some dank dungeon.

The watchman's horse spooked at a flitting robin, jumping sideways and almost throwing the heavy man to the ground. He managed to stay aboard and was distracted enough that he finally looked at my face.

"I'm lookin' for somethin' what the Starkeeper lost. He thinks he dropped it near the archery range. You seen anythin' what don't belong to you?"

"Such as?" I asked, backing Firefly away.

The guard's eyes were tracing the length of my bare leg again. When he got up as high as my hemline, he continued north, and that's when he saw it. "Like 'at!" he shouted, pointing at the amulet. "Thief! You're comin' wit' me!"

He reached out and snatched my skirt, and a horrific rip screamed across the silk until I was yanked off balance and he was able to grab my wrist. Myriam was going to kill me!

"Don't even think about runnin', wench, ye'll not get far."

"Take it! I didn't know it belonged to Starkeeper Rowan!" I tried to unpin it with one hand, but he shook me hard and I had to grab Firefly's mane to avoid falling.

"Well, weren't it obvious enough that no filthy Pyxie would have such a fancy bauble? Even one as fancy as you! Thief, 'at's what you are."

He rode me straight down the main marketplace lane, parading me past my people like some kind of criminal. I felt sick when I saw Glyn and Seraphina step out of the Bellamy Jewels stall, her looking as giddy as ever, him looking puzzled about the ruffly, beribboned girl

who was being dragged on my horse toward Rockwall.
I couldn't even look at him. I wanted to die.

CHAPTER 21

I was probably the first Pyxie to ever see what was on other side of the Rockwall gate. Under the circumstances it was no privilege. A hand-shaped bruise ached on my arm where the watchman gripped much harder than necessary as he led me and Firefly clopping along the cobblestone walk toward the menacing tower, which loomed over the village square, crowded with Festival-goers. I felt ridiculous with my hair all done up with shiny ribbons blowing behind me, my torso and legs wrapped in ruffles and lace.

A hush, followed by a wave of overly loud whispers, crept through the crowd as we passed. I dared not look at their faces.

"Look at that horse! Have you ever seen anything like it?" "Like a black horse and a white horse smushed together to make one." "And that mane!" "Have you ever seen anything so long?" "And those feet! Like feather dusters." "Do you see its tail? It's dragging on the ground!"

Women scooped up their children as we passed, swirling them away onto the safety of the hip farthest from the road, as if proximity to me and my bizarre horse would infect them with some horrible disease.

"Do you think she's a witch?"

"Look at her clothes!"

"Stand back or she'll hex us!" In less than a second, the mood shifted from curiosity to fear, and then to fury.

"What is she doing inside our gates?"

"Dirty Pyxies aren't allowed!"

"Get her out of here!"

"That horse is not natural!" It's an Orphic demon! Look at the color of its eye!"

"It's the same as hers! She must be a witch!"

I was pelted with chunks of bread and various sugary Festival food items, and the crowd grew braver the more people joined in. We passed a pigpen, and dozens of people grabbed handfuls of mud and hurled it at me and my horse, covering my face, my hair, my fancy new clothes with muck. Others continued to pelt us with food and whatever they could get their hands on. When the watchman took a stray baguette to the side of the head, he roared, "Stop it now. Starkeeper Rowan will handle this!"

As we made our way through the courtyard, I attempted to become invisible while I picked bits of food from Firefly's mane and attempted to scrape mud off my new clothes. Part of me wanted to look around, see what Rockwall looked like from the inside, but I felt so humiliated, I kept my eye on the way Rowan Tower grew colder and taller the closer we got to it. I couldn't help but inhale the delicious scents of Festival food wafting through the air, though. It was impossible to ignore the colored flags dancing in the breeze, the music and happy squeals of children, or the quaint shoppes and cottages and window boxes filled with bright flowers tucked away against the city wall, all connected by cobbled alleyways that wound like snakes into the shadows.

"Where are you taking me?" I asked the watchman, careful to keep my eyes ahead.

"I'm taking you to the Starkeeper. He will decide what to do with you. Rowan don't take kindly to thieves."

"I'm not a thief! And he can't do anything with me. I'm the Starkeeper-in-Waiting of the Lost Realm of Pyxis. The queen won't allow it. There are global laws, even where Pyxies are concerned."

"I'll let Rowan be the judge of that." He tightened his grip on my bare arm. "He's not one for paying mind to global laws. Equuleus is different. We're our own Realm. We do things our way over here. Ain't no fancy Pyxie all done up in ribbons and fluff gonna make no difference to Rowan. A thief is a thief is a thief." The guard whipped out his sword when the crowd grew thick before us. "Outta our way! Official Starkeeper business comin' through."

The crowd parted, jeering and shouting while cowering and backing up at the sight of us. Rowan Tower stood over us like an angry giant, the imposing guards flanking the massive doors looking less so in its stark shadow.

"Call for Starkeeper Rowan. I have a thief!"

But the guards had no time to obey. Hoofbeats clattered down the cobblestones behind us. The watchman turned his horse in a circle, dragging me and Firefly around the outside, until we faced the opposite direction, the galloping stallion before us parting the crowd and coming to an abrupt halt.

"What's this I hear about a Pyxie witch stealing my amulet?"

"I didn't steal it! I found it. It was on the ground. How was I to know it belonged to you?"

"Since when could a trashy Pyxie afford something so exquisite?"

"That's what I told her, Starkeeper Rowan," said the watchman, slipping off his horse and finally letting go of my arm. "Here, I got it back for you," he said stupidly, while tearing it from my purse strap.

Rowan took the amulet and turned it over, inspecting it for damage. I rubbed my bruised arm and looked for an opening in the crowd. I had to get out of Rockwall.

"What should I do with the witch, Starkeeper?"

"I told you, you'll do nothing with me! I am the Starkeeper-in-Waiting of my people. In a moon's time, I will be the Royal Starkeeper of the Lost Realm of Pyxis! The queen won't allow ill treatment of me. You've got your amulet. Let me pass." I had no idea if the queen would actually give a damn about me. Ethan Rowan looked up from his amulet and spat out a wicked laugh.

I edged Firefly forward a little, but the crowd had gathered behind the protective aura of their Starkeeper, leaving no space to weasel through. I looked past their heads, toward the gate, mentally calculating how long it would take to get there at a full gallop. Not too long. But the watchmen. They would never open the gate for me. Firefly stamped his hooves, antsy.

"How cute. A Pyxie Starkeeper. I thought your people had some crazy old crone looking after you from a ridiculous sailboat somewhere in the Silver Sea? Aren't you a bit young to take on such an… important duty?" The sarcasm dripping from "important" set me off. I knew I shouldn't bash his horse, but I couldn't help it. It was all the ammunition I had.

"Aren't YOU a little young to run an entire Realm from the back of that flea-bitten excuse for a horse?"

"Don't you dare speak ill of my steed. This is the finest stallion on the entire continent! Do you have any idea what this horse is worth?"

Firefly took this opportunity to whinny and toss his head, flinging his wild mane into an impressive arcing wave of black and white hair.

Rowan realized that it was I, in fact, who was sitting on the finest stallion on the entire continent. Probably the entire world. His face screwed into an ugly shape. "Your punishment for stealing my amulet is to relinquish your horse to me. Now!"

"I won't!" I shouted, urging Firefly into gear. We plowed past the young Starkeeper and the crowd scattered as we thundered down the square.

"Stop them!" Rowan's horse was on our heels as we sped toward the gate in the distance. "Stop this instant!"

But we ran. Musicians, children, jesters, jugglers and merchants leapt out of our way as we careened through their stalls, careful not to knock anything over. Rowan was hardly so polite; I heard carts crashing, pottery smashing and frightened shouts behind us.

We veered left and charged down the center of the road toward the huge metal gate.

"Open the gate!" I screamed, and Firefly switched into a full gallop. As we flew toward the gate with no intentions of stopping, the watchmen looked bewildered, and upon seeing their Starkeeper hot on our heels, cranked the chains to let all of us through.

We didn't stop—Firefly squeezed through the gate when the opening was barely wide enough to pass. Rowan was right behind us, shouting all manner of obscenities, extremely tactless given his royal title.

Aggie stood in the middle of the meadow, her small body creating a presence so large that both Firefly and Rowan's horse skidded to a halt without being asked, grass and dirt spraying her feet.

"What is the trouble here, Starkeeper Rowan?" Her voice was loud, scratchy, familiar. "Why do you chase our Starkeeper-in-Waiting, shouting such revolting words?"

"She stole my amulet! She deserves to get locked up in my dungeon!" Ethan Rowan screeched like an ornery teenager who had just been scolded by his parents.

"Where is this amulet now?" asked Aggie, cool as a winter night in the Percheron Mountains.

Rowan's face flushed red with fury. He wouldn't take his eyes off Firefly.

"It's here," he said, fumbling with his reins to show Aggie the jeweled bauble.

"Then our business is done. Your property has been returned to you. Good day, Starkeeper Rowan. Move along."

Rowan looked confused as Aggie's words sunk in. He shook his head, as if attempting to clear his mind of a fog, and trained his eyes back on Firefly. "But the horse. I must have that horse," he mumbled. "What do you want for it?" he asked, digging into the purse at his hip. "I'll give you any amount you ask."

"My horse is not for sale," I said, rounding Firefly's flank to Aggie's side.

"You have a fine stallion there, Starkeeper Rowan. And you can purchase another on Everday. Now, you must go back to your Festival. Your people are waiting," commanded Aggie.

Starkeeper Rowan blinked a few times, rubbed his head as if it wasn't working properly and nodded. "Yeah, okay," he agreed. He clucked at his horse and it whipped around, whisking him back through the gate to Rockwall, where his people waited and cheered. The gates slammed shut and Aggie grabbed hold of my ankle, squeezing it twice as hard as the guard had squeezed my arm.

"Ouch!" I yelped.

"Jesobel Vine. If you EVER do anything like that again, I won't be able to help you. Do you have any idea what sort of jeopardy you just put all of us in?"

But I was too impressed with how she handled Rowan to notice or care. "How did you do that?"

"If you ever paid any attention whatsoever to your studies, you'd know. It was a simple befuddlement." Aggie stomped away, but not without giving me the look of ten thousand hexes first.

"I didn't do anything!" I stormed after her. "Does this mean I'm not going to graduate?" I asked, but she ignored me.

"What have I always taught you about finding things that don't belong to you?" she snapped.

"To find the owner and return it," I sulked, suddenly eager to change out of my now completely torn and soiled clothes.

"Indeed. And why didn't you do that?"

"I don't know!"

I didn't know. The more I thought about it, the less sense it made for me to keep that creepy thing. What was my problem?

But now would probably be a terrible time to tell her about the appearance of Vallax, or that the amulet with the power to summon him was now in the clutches of a dark magic dabbler. Again, apparently.

In the back of my mind, unanswered questions tumbled around like grains of sand on an oyster's tongue.

CHAPTER 22

After the Pyxies packed up their wares, a process executed surprisingly fast given the elaborate temporary village they erected, they gathered around the stunning wagon my uncle had built for me to witness the unveiling. I stood on the bottom step of the ladder, the only bit of the wagon not covered by the huge sailcloth, still covered in mud, and somehow the sorry sight of me warmed the crowd to me in a way I hadn't yet experienced.

"One, two, three!" everyone shouted, and the sailcloth slipped away like a snake shedding its dull skin to reveal its metallic scales. I stood in awe amidst cheers and whistles. It was the most beautiful thing I had ever seen.

Firefly, carved and gilded perfectly above the door, would protect me in all of our travels, charmed to do so by Aggie.

I ran my fingers across my stallion's little golden doppelganger, and saw that Myriam had set a sparkling jewel at his brow and three small jewels on his chest, which echoed the constellation of Pyxis.

"It's magnificent! I honestly can't believe this is my very own wagon. Uncle Fin, you've outdone yourself!" I threw my arms around him.

A crowd of admirers lingered to ooh and ahh and shout birthday wishes until the twilight fairyworks began, drawing their attention away from my new home to the showers of colored lights in the sky. The unveiling was a huge success, and the reality of my destiny was just now starting to fully hit me.

I stepped inside my wagon, heady with the scent of freshly carved and painted wood, and was greeted by opulent fabrics covering the entire ceiling, the cushions, bed, pillows, and the little windows above the berth. Shimmering curtains trimmed with light-catching beads framed the bed with gorgeous handcrafted silk tassels.

"Myriam! These are Andromedan linens and curtains and Casseiopean beads. What were you thinking?"

Myriam blushed, and hurried to explain herself. "You will be our Starkeeper, Jessa. You can't go around in an ordinary wagon. We all saved up and pitched in. All of us." She made a sweeping gesture with her arm, and I knew that she meant every single Pyxie at the marketplace had given what they could to help buy only the finest materials for my wagon. My eyes pooled with tears.

I was struck by how shallow I'd been to wish for a simple life. My people cared. They cared to have a Starkeeper. And they cared that it was me who had been chosen for this duty. I was so touched I wanted to cry. I hugged Myriam and the tears slipped down my cheeks, etching rivers through the mud.

The carvings, the beautiful paint in so many gorgeous warm colors, the gold leaf flashing in the lamplight, the china cabinet full of gold-rimmed plates and cups and saucers... all of it. It was just too much! I didn't even have words. "Uncle Fin..." I squeaked, touching a border of quickbane blossoms carved into a cupboard.

"Come on, Jessa. Let's get your things from Aggie's wagon and move you in, shall we?" All I could do was follow him. It was really happening. I was leaving tonight. The next time I saw this Festival, a year from now, I would officially be the Royal Starkeeper of my people.

I honestly couldn't imagine what that meant. I was terrified, but comforted that I would begin my journey in a home that was filled with the love of my people.

When we arrived at Aggie's wagon, she had a beautiful little cake ready for me and there were a few wrapped gifts on a folding table set up in the grass. Her illumins, all ninety-eight of them, lit up the table—the effect was magical—dancing lights flashed and bobbed around in the air. The little spark fairies were so tiny, it was a wonder they could produce so much light.

As I looked at this scene, at Aggie risking her freedom to hover sixteen enchanted flames over the cake, something inside of me changed. The resistance I had carried in my heart for so long began to melt away. Some part of me was beginning to accept and even embrace my fate. A sliver of excitement grew inside my heart, and a sliver of pride. A new resolve. I would pour my heart into my studies with Starkeeper Yarrow. I would do right by my people. I would find a way to lead them home, find a way to shape a good ending to the awful legend. And I was suddenly sorry for paying such disrespect to Aggie for all of the time she'd sacrificed to train me.

"Jesobel, I need to speak with you." Aggie's voice was so serious, my heart began to race, my mind to tumble over all of the things I'd been hiding from her. I wasn't ready to get in trouble for all of that. Not now. Not after I finally made a promise to myself to do right by my people. I broke out in a nervous sweat, and waited for Aggie to lay into me.

"What is it, Aggie?" I asked, not really wanting to know.

Aggie approached me and fastened a small golden charm onto the Ghostmoth Hex's chain, stamped with the Magic Weaver sigil.

"Congratulations, Jessa. You've graduated to Magic Weaver." Aggie's eyes were rimmed with tears as she called my spark fairies out, and drew the Magic Weaver sigil into my quickflame.

"I can't believe I did it!" I whispered, rubbing the charm between my finger and thumb.

"Neither can I." Aggie laughed, and I melted at hearing the sound of it for the first time in ever so long.

"So that's it? I'm a Magic Weaver now?" I grinned, surprised at how elated and proud I felt.

"Yep, that's it!" She smiled. "You're all ready to continue training with Starkeeper Yarrow."

I breathed a sigh of relief, and Myriam led my family in a Pyxie birthday song while I blew out the flames—they were tricky to catch and everyone was laughing by the time I finally had to extinguish them with a counter-enchantment, after chasing them around the wagon three times, huffing and puffing like a crazed bleakhound. Aggie, Fin and Myriam give me a round of applause and handed me their gifts one by one.

Lost in this tiny moment of cheer, it almost seemed like any other birthday, but then I paused, and drank in the faces I loved so dearly and etched them into my heart. The faces I wouldn't see for a year or more once we parted ways at the Seven Bridges Road. Some Pyxies would go on to wander the continent, others would continue even farther around the globe during the winter months by boat. The seafaring Pyxies, whose sailboats were every bit as colorful and finely crafted as our wagons, would meet back here with their exotic wares in thirteen moons. But my small family would not sail, nor travel far. They would stay close and travel the borderland festivals, taking orders for wagons, administering remedies, selling linens and skirts, and stopping in to visit Liam and his herd of horses in Sugar Hollow.

My heart crumbled with nostalgia, but I couldn't let them see it. I could see in their eyes that they needed me to be strong. I kissed each cheek, and thanked them for the thoughtful gifts: From Myriam, an understated silky violet skirt (with the fashionable Orion hemline) a stunning soft blouse in a miraculous shade of cream made of fine Andromedan silk, and a beautifully embroidered, fit-for-a-Starkeeper satin corset, with a leather arm guard and new gatherings bag to match.

"The leather things are from Liam. I whipped the clothes up today. I know those fancy things just really aren't you, are they?" she said, apologetically. "And it's a good thing I did, seeing how fast you managed to ruin your coronation outfit!" She laughed.

"I'm so sorry I ruined this outfit, Myriam, but I do love the new clothes, they're absolutely perfect!"

Franci and the triplets left a fragrant box of sticky cinnamon buns, and there was a delicate muslin bag filled with incense and Zola's soaps that must have been from Glyn. I tried not to feel the sadness that lurked in my chest about his absence.

Aggie approached me with liquid eyes and her mouth pulled into a taught line that must have helped hold her tears back. She grabbed my right hand and said nothing, but I could see a thousand thoughts flickering through her eyes. It was as if she was scanning me for some sort of final assessment, some confirmation that she had done her job well. I tried to muster up the mature look of a student who had just graduated with perfect marks, and let that show through in my eyes. I wanted her to be proud of me. I realized I was holding my breath when Aggie let a smile creep across her face, and whispered, "I'm so very proud of you, Jessa."

I exhaled, relieved, and gave her a hug. When she pulled away, she was holding a wooden box. I lifted the lid and inside was a beautiful lacy cuff with a chain of stones linked to my mother's ring. The stones were a mysterious color, almost gray and lifeless. Somewhat ugly, in fact. I was startled, and awed, because the gold shone in the moonlight so beautifully where it cradled the lackluster gems.

"This also belonged to your mother, Jessa," she said, placing a golden wreath of quickbane branches on my head. "She would have been the next Starkeeper, you know. She would be very proud of you."

My heart did some sort of weirdly uncomfortable gymnastic twist behind my ribs and I swallowed down a lump in my throat. I didn't know what to say. I had no idea my mother was to be the Starkeeper. I guess it made sense, but I was stung that nobody ever told me. That Aggie never told me. More secrets? What other secrets had she kept? I scanned her face suspiciously, but if she was hiding anything else, she was too good at it. She just looked like Aggie, and finally an Aggie who was proud of me. I shook off the weird feeling and gave her a squeeze. I never knew my mother anyway. Aggie had been the only parent I'd ever known.

"Thank you, Aggie," I said, feeling the weight of the circlet on my head.

"You'll need to wear that now, until you trade it for your crown at the Ice Palace, okay?"

"I will. I promise," I said striking a royal pose. Everyone laughed when they realized how muddy I still was, and how ridiculous the golden circlet looked on my wild, mud-caked hair.

Aggie whispered, "Your actions will change the fate of the world, Jesobel, try to be mindful so that the change will be a good one." She gave my hand a final squeeze and disappeared into her wagon. I imagined the time had come for her tears to fall.

Fin walked me back to my new wagon with his arm around my shoulders, and helped me carry my small armful of belongings.

"You're going to do fine, Jessa. You'll make one heck of a Starkeeper," he said with a smile. But his voice was gravelly and I could tell he was trying to keep a lid on his own tears. All of this emotion was making me feel like my body was made of the ever-sloshing sea.

"I made this for you," he said, pulling something out of his pocket as we stood in front of my new steps. I inhaled the scent of fresh wood and paint. "I didn't know what else to give you."

I took it in my hand, and wrapped my arms around him. "Uncle Fin. I'm really going to miss you." I couldn't cry. I wouldn't. I wouldn't let him worry about me. I would be fine. It was only a year, really, and then I could come back and see everyone, at least during the Festival before my Starkeeper duties called me away to govern other pockets of Pyxies around the globe.

"I'm going to miss you too, Jessa. See you at Seven Bridges Road, right? This isn't goodbye quite yet!"

"Right," I said, turning Fin's gift over and over in my hands. Leave it to Uncle Fin to give me the most thoughtful gift of all. "I better hitch up, then." I smiled. But when Fin walked away, I climbed my stairs and let the tears come down. Why hadn't Glyn bothered to show up for my party?

CHAPTER 23

Sobbing quietly, I packed my things inside my wagon, awkwardly shifting them from cupboard to cupboard, not really knowing where anything should go. I knew Aggie's wagon with my eyes closed. This one felt so foreign to me, no matter its extraordinary beauty.

I imagined a month's travel in it would make it begin to feel like home. But then I'd have to leave it at the harbor and retrieve it when I returned a year later, and it would feel foreign all over again. Myriam had made beautiful soft towels for me, and I felt wretched wiping mud all over them, but I was still a wreck from my unplanned visit with Rowan and I just needed to be clean. I decided to ride over to the spring and bathe. I figured I should probably change my clothes and begin my journey playing the part of Starkeeper-to-Be looking my best.

I stood in the doorway and admired my wagon briefly, and a swelling of gratitude filled me up. I was so blessed. Every little detail of my wagon held the love of my people. I decided right then that I would spend every spare moment practicing the magic Aggie had worked so hard to teach me. A flash of shame washed over me again; I had been such an unworthy student. Not anymore. Whatever it took, I would be the best Starkeeper I could be for my people.

"Hey, Jessa." Glyn's deep voice startled me from my reverie. "Happy Birthday," he said, offering me a hand and a beaming smile.

There was a sparkle of sadness in his smile that ate a hole in my heart. I stepped down the stairs and let him enfold me in his arms. Glyn. The boy I would have married. The boy who would marry me still. But I could never allow him to throw away a happy Pyxie life for a wife who would rarely be at home. Besides, it just wasn't done. Pyxian Starkeepers don't marry. I realized my mind was made up about him. There was no way for us to make it work. And I was sort of okay with that. At least here, surrounded by the strength of my recent resolve.

Glyn smelled like a mixture of incense and leather, and as I buried my face into his neck, I inhaled the faint spicy scent of clove soap and breathed in the clean warmth of his skin. A little sweaty, but so familiar and comforting. In an instant, all the strength I had mustered up just seconds before drained out my feet, and I let a little sob escape before I was able to pull myself together without Glyn noticing. But he noticed.

"Aw, Jessa. It will be okay. You'll only be gone a year. And think of it. You'll be sailing on the Queen's silver ship. I mean, who gets to do that?"

We'd talked about this so many times over the years. My standard answer was "Who would want to!" But standing near my new wagon, I realized how cruel that would be to say, so I just nodded my head and snuggled deeper into his neck, and twisted a lock of his hair around my fingers. "I'm going to miss you, Glyn," I whispered. And it was all I could do to keep it together. The reality of everything was coming at me from everywhere, pressing in on me from all angles. I squeezed myself against Glyn, and felt his arms tighten protectively around me.

"Walk me to the spring?" I asked, needing to do something, anything to make this feeling stop. If I let Glyn hold me like that for one more second, I feared I might lock him in my wagon and take off past Saggita, past the harbor where the Royal Argentum awaited, and escape into the mountains or even across the sea. To anywhere, so that I might avoid my fate and keep Glyn in my arms forever. It took every ounce of strength I possessed to let go of his neck, to find his hand with mine and fish it from its warm resting spot on the small of my back. I put one foot in front of the other and pointed us in the direction of the spring. With these painful steps, my journey away from the life I had always dreamed of had truly begun. I tried to act normal.

"I need a bath. Look at me," I said, turning toward Glyn with my eyebrows up and flashed him a stupid, phony grin.

"Goodness, you are caked with mud."

"I had a pretty exciting day. I met Starkeeper Rowan." There were so many other things I'd been wanting to talk to Glyn about, but I couldn't. Not now.

"You did?" Glyn was genuinely interested. "How did that happen?"

"Oh, long story. But you know how he is notorious for his collection of the finest horses? Well, he took one look at Firefly and wanted to buy him on the spot. Offered me a fortune for him."

Glyn laughed. "He was sorely disappointed, no doubt."

"Sorely is right. I could see he was about to throw a tantrum. He's young, that Starkeeper Rowan," I pointed out. Not that it mattered. I'm young, and would have similar responsibilities soon.

"Did you see the notices, Jesobel?"

"How could I miss them?" I said, selfishly relishing the feel of his hand in mine. "They are nailed to every pole in the Marketplace. I wonder why he would banish the use of magic in this realm? It's not like Equuleus is crawling with Magic Weavers. There are only two of us." My cheeks burned when I said it. I had just admitted to being an actual Magic Weaver!

"But it's common knowledge that all Pyxies are black magic voodoo witches and warlocks!" he teased. "Seriously, you should have seen how many middlings wore talismans to ward off our 'evil' magic this year. They even bought them from Old Sully's booth! The lanes and alleys buzzed with an underlying sense of unease and mistrust. It was quite disturbing. And also slightly entertaining," he said with a chuckle.

"Really?" I had been so wrapped up with learning the Venoms Trivium that I hadn't noticed that I never had a chance to wander through the lanes and visit all of my favorite shoppes.

"You did see the bit about 'immediate imprisonment' didn't you?"

"Well, no. I mean I didn't really read the whole thing. To be honest, I thought it was a bit silly." I didn't want to admit what I heard the Starkeeper say during the windowroot charm—I had completely pushed the whole dabbling with dark magic thing out of my mind until now. I pushed it out again—there was no way he would really do that. Brothers accuse each other of all sorts of untrue things. I'd seen it a million times. But the amulet… I didn't want to think about the amulet.

Glyn stopped and whipped me around, gripping my upper arm. "You, of all people, should pay attention to what that notice says, Jessa. You have the most to lose. For instance, what if someone had seen you doing magic in those woods yesterday? Or the day before that?"

"I hadn't really thought of that as magic. I was just learning things from Aggie." I shrugged. "Plus, she was so careful. Still, I don't think it's really that big of a big deal," I said, remembering how easily I had distracted the watchman with moonblossom oil, and how Aggie had befuddled Rowan without him even noticing. I tried to walk toward the spring, but he caught my arm again.

"You were learning *magic*, Jesobel! And from the looks of that notice, Starkeeper Rowan is serious about cracking down on the use of magic in his realm. Does 'immediate imprisonment' seriously mean nothing to you? You're about to become our Starkeeper, Jesobel. You need to be more careful."

"Hm." I shrugged, a little annoyed. "It's not like we go around shooting sparks from our eyes. He'll never know. If there was really anything to worry about, Aggie wouldn't have ignited my birthday candles." *Or used a befuddlement charm on Starkeeper Rowan, I remembered, still impressed.*

"Just be careful, okay?" The stern concern oozing from his voice was just so dramatic.

"Fine! I will."

"You better," Glyn warned, and planted a kiss on my forehead before allowing me to keep walking.

The big moon, Alcyone, sat heavy and full, still low in the deepening twilight, her eldest child peeking up over the horizon below her. Behind us, the fairyworks exploded and streaked through the sky, bursting into illuminating scenes animated by spark fairies assembled in shapes of creatures of every mythical sort. I guess Starkeeper Rowan made an exception for the magic used in the fairyworks show, or maybe he didn't even realize that spark fairies were magic, or that Pyxie fairyworks were actual acrobatic spark fairies being shot out of cannons and not some fiery explosives.

An enormous glittering winged horse circled out of the light show and whooshed over our heads, doing a dramatic dance of fancy maneuvers, and then disappeared into the moon in a shower of twinkling lights. An impressive river of spark fairies zoomed back past us to assemble themselves inside a cannon to form another mythical light beast after the blast.

"I can't believe we aren't watching the show." A little too much disappointment leaked out in my voice, and I hoped I didn't sound whiny. It was just Glyn, but still. I was supposed to be acting like a Royal Starkeeper now, not moping because I was missing the fairyworks. Glyn squeezed my hand and led me to the edge of the spring. The moon's liquid double shimmered on the water's dark surface, framed by bursts of colored fairylights reflecting down from the sky.

"Look, see? Not missing a thing," Glyn crooned.

"Tell me you have soap in your pocket." I laughed, knowing he did. Glyn always had soap in his pocket, because Zola had an insane habit of cramming a new bar into his pocket every day. "And tell me it doesn't smell like a man," I pleaded.

But I knew that it would. Ever since Glyn turned sixteen, his mom stopped filling his pockets with the sweet, vanilla- and fruit-scented soaps that reeked of happy Pyxie children far and wide, and began tucking bars of dusky, spiced clove-and licorice-and rum-scented soaps into his pockets. *You just never know when you might need a good bar of soap,* Zola always said.

Glyn had a habit of carving these soaps into little animals and giving them away to Pyxie children. If he didn't, he'd have cartfuls of soap to tote around. How Zola thought a person could ever use that much soap was beyond me, but I had to admit, Glyn did always smell really nice.

"Jessa," said Glyn, his voice throaty and low. He snaked his fingers between mine and turned me to face him, pressing a hand on the small of my back. The space between our bodies became palpable, and I grew nervous, fearing he was about to kiss me again. And secretly hoping he would, and that that stupid redhead was watching us. And then scolding myself for such thoughts. I dug for my resolve, not so easy to do as it was a few minutes ago.

He gazed at me with those blue-green eyes that felt like home the way nothing else did. I saw my entire childhood dancing in their depths, as they made tiny movements back and forth, recording and memorizing my mud-caked face. Glyn's hand slipped from my back and he reached into his pocket without taking his eyes from my own.

"For you," he whispered, and handed me a small gift, wrapped in thin petal-pressed paper and tied with a pale purple silk ribbon. He lifted it to my nose and I inhaled. Jasmine. My mother's flower, infused into a bar of soap! I'd only smelled jasmine oil once in my entire life. Glyn was with me the day that wealthy woman visited Zola's shoppe at the Saggita Harvest Festival, her perfume an intoxicating blend of sweet violet jasmine and bright white jasmine blossoms. She was looking for jasmine soap, but Zola didn't have any.

"Oh, Glyn, how did Zola ever find it?" Jasmine was so rare, so expensive and so hard to acquire. It was the next rarest flower to the singing Aria blossom, whose perfume was so outrageously priced that it was practically a mythical legend. I was stunned. I didn't know what to say.

"Take it. Open it." Glyn smiled, and I felt his hand shaking in mine. Why was he so nervous? I gave his hand a squeeze, tucked a stray lock of hair behind his ear, and planted a little kiss on his cheek.

"Please thank Zola for me, from the bottom of my heart." I saw Glyn's cheeks turn pink and he fidgeted uncomfortably.

"It's not from my mother, Jessa. It's from me. My mother doesn't know anything about this." He uncurled my fingers and placed the wrapped soap on my palm. "Please, open it."

Now it was my turn to have pink cheeks. "You... made this, Glyn? But how ... where... did you get the jasmine...?" I reached into his pocket and dug out his man-soap. "I can't use it right now! I need to save it. It's *jasmine*, Glyn!"

I went to tuck the soap away into my muddy purse, but before I was able to place it inside, Glyn stole it from me and said, "Open it. Please." And he looked a little mad as he slapped the package back into my palm.

"Okay, okay. Do I really smell that bad?" I smiled, but his somber eyes did not register my attempt to amuse him.

I tugged one end of the ribbon and a loop snaked away. I pulled the other and flipped the soap over to unwrap the folds of delicate paper. The top of the swirly lavender and white soap had been intricately carved into a cluster of tiny star jasmine blossoms nestled on delicate leaves. Embedded in the center of the little bouquet was a circle of golden metal. I swallowed my heart, and trembled, completely terrified to look at Glyn, who, in a swift, graceful movement was down on his knee, peering up at my face. I couldn't hide the horror in my eyes when they met his. I was not prepared for this. This was not part of the plan. He cleared his throat. I tried not to die.

"Jesobel Vine, I have known you all your life, and I have loved you since the first time you pulled my hair." He saw me dying, he saw that I was nauseated, and that I wished he would just shut up. And I hated that I was hurting him. I was about to hurt him beyond repair. I thought I could slip away with an easy hug, maybe one goodbye kiss, but he was ruining everything.

"Jesobel, I know that as Starkeeper you will have duties that take you away from me. But I can't bear the thought of a life without you in it. If missing you for months on end will result in my wife returning to me, even for only the tiniest stretches, I can bear it. We can have children and they can keep me company until their mother returns for a spell. Please, Jessa, I beg you to be my wife. Promise your heart to mine. You know we are meant to be. I will wait for you. I will be here for you when you return, and we can marry next year, on your birthday. I've already asked Fin and Aggie for your hand. He and Myriam and Aggie are overjoyed. Aggie knows that if anyone can make this work, it's us. Please say you'll be mine." The green of his eyes was as vibrant as I'd ever seen it. The way his dark lashes curled up at me should have made my heart flutter, but my throat tightened and I could scarcely breathe.

I was angry and sad and touched and I wanted to kiss him and hold him and punch him and push him away all at once. How could he be so thoughtless? How could he ask me to do what I'd spent the past two years convincing myself I wouldn't? I wouldn't be his absent wife. I wouldn't make him live a lonely existence and feel like half a man. He needed a woman by his side. That redhead. Or any of the girls who had taken to following him around with butterfly eyelashes and rouge-kissed cheeks. He could choose anyone. Why would he choose me? Why would Aggie agree to this? She knew about the compass!

I stood dumbstruck, my solid existence losing its final foothold in the world I had always known, and I tumbled into oblivion. I handed him the soap and the ring and dropped to my knees and began splashing water on my muddy face to buy time. I needed time for this mess of unruly thoughts inside my head to stop plummeting down into the groundless depths of uncertainty. I needed the water to shock me back to here and now, to give me the words that wouldn't shatter Glyn's heart. But those words didn't exist. I knew it. And he was about to know it.

I hated him for making me do this. We talked about this. About how I would not take a husband. There was a reason that Pyxian Starkeepers don't marry. They do have children, but those situations are arranged. A late-night visitor in a pitch-black candle-less room. Names are not exchanged, and neither are glances, but nine months later a baby is born. That was my lot in life. That was my fate. That is the only way a Pyxian Starkeeper traditionally procreates. Glyn knew this. How could he be so cruel to dangle this carrot of a life before me, this perfect life that can never remotely be mine?

Before I knew it, I was stripping my clothes off and diving into the spring in my bloomers and camisole, scrubbing my flesh vigorously with the man-soap I stole from Glyn's pocket. He must have thought me insane; his heart must have been cracking into irreparable shards. Was it my fault or his? Either way, I felt awful. I tried to make it look like I just wanted to be clean before I gave him my answer, but I was only fooling myself.

"Jesobel," I heard him squeak. And then there was a splash and he was wrapping his arms around me and pulling me close, and I was thrashing against his gentle touch like a wild kitten who didn't want to be bathed. His chest was bare, and his hair framed his face, landing sexily on his perfect cheekbones, which were dotted with droplets of water from my thrashing, like tiny wet diamonds. I gave up and went boneless, dissolving into him with a heart so heavy it could sink a ship if one were tethered to it. I loved Glyn so much it hurt. I never wanted to admit it. Admitting it was just asking for unfathomable pain.

"My wild Pyxie girl," he crooned, pushing soggy strands of hair from my face. My heart hammered in my chest, so hard that I could feel it beating against Glyn's with angry fists.

"Don't, Glyn. I can't. I can't do this..." I avoided his eyes. I tried not to notice the way his long lashes curled up at the ends, making his sea-colored eyes sparkle the way the sun does on the lilting, boat-rocking swells at Saggita Harbor.

Glyn wiped dirt from my nose with his thumb and the electricity of that simple touch was going to kill me. I was certain that I would be dead momentarily. I simply couldn't handle the thousand conflicting thoughts and emotions pulling me apart, all heightened to impossible agony with the slightest touch of his tender hand.

I turned my head back toward the market lanes. It was almost all broken down, and caravans would be lining up at the gate soon. My wagon stood alone, ridiculous swaths of gold leaf gleaming in the rising moonlight, and flashing under the booming light show in the sky. Firefly grazed near a front wheel, patiently awaiting the beginning of our new life together. Beyond, I could see Fin and Myriam hitching a horse to Aggie's wagon, and Pennyfeathers wandered over to Firefly. The fairyworks were ramping up to the big finale and the multitude of explosions popping off high above us mirrored the panicky implosions bursting behind my ribcage.

I took a deep breath, and kept my eyes on my wagon. My new life. My fate. Which did not include Glyn, no matter how much I wished it could. I couldn't agree to his crazy idea. I couldn't be the wife who made him miserable by never being home. Or by starting an Orphic war... I wanted to give him the kiss that truly belonged to his wife, but if I did, I knew it would hurt us both. And it wouldn't be fair of me to take that from him, or from his future wife. Even if it was that stupid redhead.

When I let him kiss me at the harbor last autumn, it was awkward and passionless, though sweet. Living without Glyn wasn't a reality yet, and I guess I took him for granted in many ways. And somehow I knew that a kiss wouldn't be anything like that now. It would be amazing, and packed with a lifetime of love and years of future longing, it would make the wild sky-high explosions above us pale in comparison. But it would break us both, and make it impossible for him to choose another. Which he must do. As much as I hated the idea, I knew it was true. It would be asking too much to expect him to live his life without a real Pyxie wife.

My body trembled against Glyn, the cold and the overwhelming emotions had set me to shivering and my skin was a mass of gooseflesh. The water pooled at my ribs, chilling my bones. Glyn didn't seem to notice that he was still in his trousers and that they were soaked to the waist.

"Glyn, you are my best friend in the world. You know that. You know I love you. So much." My teeth were chattering so hard, I hoped that he could understand what I was saying. I put my cheek on his chest so I didn't have to see his eyes when I said it. "But I can't be your wife."

The jasmine soap was on the ground, and of course this was where my gaze naturally landed. I felt sick as my eyes traced the circle of gold embedded in the blossoms. The fairyworks ended in a final huge explosion, and the oohs and ahhs grew loud enough to hear from where we were, way over by the cliff side of the meadow, where the stream that feeds the spring continues away down the valley, eventually falling over the massive cliff and emptying into the sea.

And then there was nothing but dead, cold silence aside from the sound of Glyn's heart thumping against my cheek, and my own nervous teeth-chattering breaths. A massive swarm of giant butterflies swirled above our heads and away into the moonlight, finishing in a shower of sparkles. The show was over.

Glyn's arms tightened around me, and my body mashed into his. He put his cheek on top of my head and his hand moved slowly from my waist to my hips, up my side, over my shoulder, to the back of my neck, and then stopped, cradling my head. My vision went dark as I felt his hand guiding my head to turn and face him so that his lips hovered near mine, and his breath heated the space between us.

"Jesobel. How can you deny this? How?" Glyn's voice was deeper than I'd ever heard it sound. He searched my eyes for confirmation that I felt the way he did. I knew he'd find it, so I fought to hide it. I looked away, but he made me look back. I closed my eyes.

"Just look at me, and tell me you don't love me, and that you don't want to be my wife." His voice was desperate. His touch told me he was certain I felt the same way, but there was a hairline thread of terror hidden in the shadows of his voice, and this terror was what woke me from wanting to blurt out that I did love him, and that I wanted to be his wife. That I couldn't live without him, and that we *could* make it work. This sliver of terror trumped the fantasy. It *was* just a fantasy that we belonged together and that I could somehow find a way to make him happy as his globe-trotting, never-at-home, Dream Weaver, Starkeeper, Heart of Azimuth, Way-Bringer wife.

Thank Ariah for that terror, because it gave me the strength to do what I knew I must. As my eyes met his, and his sweet breath played on my lips and made its way into my lungs with each nervous inhale, and as he moved to fill that minuscule space between us, his lips pressing gently and deliciously on mine, I forced myself to drop my eyes and turn away. His kiss skittered across my cheek and clumsily landed somewhere near my ear with an exasperated breath that sent unwanted tingles down my spine.

I clung to Glyn. I squeezed him as tight as I could, fighting the urge to give in to those wild emotions. I wanted him so bad it was killing me, but I couldn't have him. If I truly loved him, and I truly did, I couldn't have him. He must find another wife. I held him until I accepted that no matter how hard I squeezed, I wouldn't become part of him in the way either of us wished I could. And then I pushed him away with every ounce of strength I could summon, scrambled out of the stream and grabbed my muddy clothes from the ground.

He stood there, stunned and gape-mouthed, unable to register what just happened. I picked the ring from the soap as he slowly digested my cruel actions. As he climbed out of the stream with a look in his eyes that would haunt me for the rest of my life, I loosened the circle of gold from its soapy coffin and pushed it into his palm. I looked deep into his eyes and told the biggest lie I would ever utter.

"Glyn, I don't love you that way. I don't want to be your wife." And before he could grab my wrist to stop me, I turned and ran, leaving my jasmine-scented heart scattered in a million pieces at his feet.

CHAPTER 24

I reached my beautiful new wagon, sobbing, breathless, and pounded up the ladder, shoved my way inside and locked the door behind me.

If Glyn followed me, I won't let him in. I can't let him in. It's done. I have to just go.

I shimmied out of my wet underthings, scrubbed myself dry with a lovely, soft towel and slipped into new bloomers. I quickly ran a brush through my hair once I found it—I hid it from myself in a random drawer while hastily unpacking—and then put on my new clothes and my mother's circlet and ring, glad for the strength they gave me to remember my one and only job from here on out.

When it was time to put the stairs away, check supplies and hitch up Firefly, I peeked through a crack in the door, fearing—and maybe even hoping—I would see Glyn, but he was not there.

The burnt, metallic scent of expired fairyworks wafted through the air while smoky, ghostlike anemones littered the purpling sky above like a spectral coral reef drifting near a blanket of fat, low clouds that looked dark and heavy with rain.

The last ray of sun had long vanished behind the distant hills, and the wagon was more or less ready to leave Rowan Tower's grounds, despite my clumsy fumbling with every task set before me. By the time

I was brave enough to step out of my wagon and hitch up Firefly, Glyn was nowhere to be seen. Caravans were already heading out. A long line of painted wagons snaked toward the northwest gate. I was glad for it, but a gaping hole in my chest let the wind whistle through it, punctuating its emptiness and shameful sorrow that Glyn didn't try to follow me. I shouldn't have wished that he had, but part of me did.

I wrestled with a complicated knot Fin had tied to Firefly's halter. I tried to console my broken heart by conjuring the anger that still lurked at the edges of my loss. How dare Glyn buy expensive jasmine and make me soap with it! How dare he carve dainty blossoms on it! How dare he nestle a ring into those blossoms! And how *dare* he propose to me! I worked myself into a comforting fury as I fought with the stupid knot. Firefly stood patiently by, chewing a hank of grass.

I didn't know how long he'd been standing there when I felt the tingle of being watched, and I startled, noticing the same skinny, dirty boy from earlier in the week. He lurked at my side and fidgeted, with eyes that would not meet mine.

"Oh, hello there." I flashed an irritated smile, and returned to consuming thoughts of Glyn, while tugging at the tight coils.

Evening faded to night and the boy silently watched me work at the knot. The tiny copper bells on my ankles tinkled with my movements, and somehow the harmonious sounds, along with the boy's silence, heightened my frustration.

The boy stared openly at my bust in the rising moonlight. My cleavage was framed in golden embroidery the same hue as Glyn's hair. Myriam was a master at her craft. I vaguely wished Glyn could see me in these new clothes, rather than the muddy purple confection from earlier, and then I scolded myself for having such thoughts. *You just ruined him*, I reminded myself, sick with the truth of it. *You'll be lucky if he ever wants to speak to you again.*

The boy licked his lips before he spoke, never taking his lusty gaze from my cleavage. He hadn't behaved so rudely the first time we met, and I suddenly felt like putting an arrow through him, which reminded me that I'd forgotten my bow and arrows in Aggie's wagon, which was probably long gone. I'd have to get them at the Seven Bridges Road. My fingers worked the knot, but my mind was acutely aware of the way my blouse draped a little too low, and the way it might reveal the hole where my heart once existed, and how I didn't need this boy nosing into the business of my suffering. I wished he would just leave.

"What do you want?" I snapped. Aggie would be appalled at my curtness. I didn't care. He was irritating. Thunder rumbled ominously in the distance.

"M'Liy-dee, Lard Rowan has ardered me to parchase yar harse. I brung you a parse." He extended his arm and dropped a fancy leather pouch, heavy with golden mollusks in front of my face, without waiting for me to accept it. As it plummeted, I caught it and hurled it right back at him, a little too forcefully. It thumped him square in the chest.

"Ooof," he grunted, and the pouch fell to the ground with a metallic thud.

"I told Starkeeper Rowan I don't want his money, and he can't have my horse. You go tell him I appreciate his offer, but I politely decline, or something like that. Something one would say to a Royal Starkeeper. Now, go. Get out of here." I gave the boy a disgusted glare, shooed him away and went back to untying my knot, while other, uncomfortable knots gathered and tightened in my gut.

The boy didn't budge from his spot. He shifted his weight back and forth, fidgeting until I glared up at him a final time just as the knot came free.

It was at this moment that our eyes locked, and his surprise was as great as mine when his skinny arm darted like a snake to snatch the rope from my hand. Quick as a sparrow, he turned and ran, dragging Firefly behind him. In a fraction of an instant, the boy was clumsily aboard Firefly's bare back. He floundered with the wagon reins and flopped like a ragdoll as Firefly bucked wildly, but the boy displayed his skill as a horseman and managed to gain control, despite Firefly's best efforts to unseat him.

With a screeching neigh of protest issuing from Firefly's peeled-back lips, the pair thundered toward the Rockwall gate and Rowan's castle a league and a half down the meadow.

"Dirty little tramp! Nobody steals my horse!" Venomous hate poisoned my veins, pumping from my heart to my fingertips until I trembled all over and swallowed down an unladylike curse before it flew from my lips. I was already mad, but now I was blind with fury.

Without thinking, I dug into the pouch at my hip, snatching up the tiny cobalt vial of viperberry beetle venom, companion to the hex I had learned two days before, and hadn't paid very close attention to *as usual*, Aggie would say. I hoped I could remember the words. I repeated them ten thousand times that day. I leapt onto Pennyfeathers, who Myriam left as a travel companion for Firefly, and charged after my stolen horse, screaming after the boy with a fury I had never felt in my life. I was no longer consumed by thoughts of Glyn or my bleak, loveless future without him—all I cared about was getting my horse back.

Firefly was fast, and that skinny boy struggled to control him. An experienced rider, clearly, but maybe out of his league. They struggled with each other, Firefly doing his best to ignore the boy's commands and turn back to me, the boy muscling the long driving reins as he kicked at Firefly's ribs. Firefly bucked and kicked, but the scrawny boy would not dislodge. Perhaps he was not out of his league, after all. I decided right then that I hated that dirty boy.

I tore after them, wild-eyed and ready, down the meadowy hillside toward the Rockwall gate. I repeated the hex in my mind over and over and over, the words keeping cadence with Penny's drumming hooves. My eyes began to flash with quickflame, the heat surging through them as I urged my mount forward, binding the hex to my tongue. Rockwall drew near. The guards at the gate took notice of the action barreling forth, and readied themselves with swords drawn.

My eyes were daggers fixed upon the boy, the boy with the audacity to steal my beloved Firefly! The gap between the two horses shrank, as did the gap between the riders and the guards. I raced to Firefly's side, revenge in my eyes, a fistful of Penny's mane in one hand, viperberry beetle vial held up high in the other.

It's just the Viperberry Hex. The least dangerous, I told myself.

But I was too angry to notice that I was summoning immense amounts of Orphic magic. The cobalt glass flashed in the rising moonlight, shadows coiling inside. The boy clung to Firefly and bounced upon his back like a toy boat caught on a raging sea, and delicious fear glittered in his dimwitted eyes. I drove Penny close enough to hear the boy's breath huffing under Firefly's heavy hoofbeats.

When we were side by side, horses bumping into one another as we galloped, I abandoned Penny's mane with my left hand, reached for Firefly's harness reins and missed. Furious, I screamed, "Look at me, thief!" and shook the blue vial at him.

But the boy did not look—he was too busy trying to keep his leg from being crushed between our horses, and attempting to steer Firefly away from me.

"Guaards! Guaaards! 'elp me!" he shouted with a pitchy cracked voice. The armored watchmen rushed out to meet the race as my mare began to tire. I dropped away, and the boy gained a nose, and then several lengths. Firefly screamed and tried to turn around, but the boy grew confident again and handled him like a master horseman. I hated him with such intensity, I seethed. The little thief dared to glance back in triumph as the gate drew near, with a wicked, crooked-toothed grin on his filthy face. *Big mistake.*

The watchmen gaped at me in awe as we came into view over

a hillock. They were unable to move. In their eyes, I knew I was an ethereal specter with midnight skirts and moonsilk blouse billowing in the wind, eyes alight with fearsome intensity—my quickflame was like a lightning storm from within. To them, I was a witch by all accounts. And forbidden from practicing magic in the realm. *Punishable by death*.

I didn't care. Nobody stole my horse. I tore the cork from the vial with my teeth as I charged the boy. I spat the cork into the wind, and thrust the hex to the velvet-blue sky. The guards watched in horror as a string of wicked words flew from my lips. Beautiful, terrible, awful, wicked words.

A slick jet stream of vapor the color of fiend's tongue shot from the cobalt vial with a deafening high-pitched shriek that neither I nor the horses could hear. The guards, however, clamped their hands over their ears, and the boy wailed as the screech pierced into their very souls.

The shrieking vapor twisted and snaked through the air, a heat-seeking, serpentine banshee locked on to its target, summoned from the venom of the viperberry beetle and its chaotic Orphic magic.

On impact, the spirit-snake twisted itself around the boy's middle, then ripped him from his seat atop Firefly and slammed him to the ground with a sickening thud. The vaporous serpent coiled tighter, squeezing life from the boy's soul, from the boy's body. He screamed like a terrified rabbit as I circled my mare tightly around him, spraying his frightened face with clumps of torn earth.

"You shouldn't have taken my horse!" I screeched down at him, something terrifyingly dark seeping through my fury and taking hold of my heart with intoxicating power.

The boy's eyes began to bulge, his fingers curled stiffly. He lay still on his back, terror contorting his face, gasping for breath in noisy, labored inhales. My veins surged with satisfied justice, as I finally grabbed hold of Firefly's bridle and pulled him close to Penny's side, breathing in his familiar scent with relief. But it was a restless relief. A false relief.

When the boy went limp, there was a silence so deep and so still, punctuated only by the heavy puffs issuing from the horses' nostrils. In that frozen moment, Aggie's voice echoed in my head, and all triumph drained instantly from my body.

"Do not use this hex unless your own life is threatened, and unless there is absolutely no alternative. Beware of absorbing its dark magic. Viperberry beetle venom can bring the most painful kind of death to any foe unlucky enough to be near for the duration of the spell. Are you listening to me, Jesobel?"

"Ohhh... Ohh, no! What have I done?" Frantic, I slipped from the mare, hurried to the boy, and put a trembling hand to his dirty pale cheek. It was cold, too cold. I looked at his unmoving limbs, and my stomach soured. *What have I done? What have I done! Please live, please do not be dead! Why didn't I pay closer attention!*

I shook him. Called to him. I even whispered my secret song to him. He smelled of straw and horse piss. His clothes were tattered and his fingernails filthy. Lifeless saucer eyes stared blankly to the sky, fear darkly frozen into them, fingers curled in petrified horror. And then there was a sickening rattle in his chest, as his final breath was sucked from his lungs. His stiff lips were blue.

I sobbed. Grief and shame flooded every last cell in my body. "I'm sorry. I'm so, so sorry... Oh, Firefly, what have I done!"

The watchmen seized me. I went wild. I kicked and screamed and scratched at the men's faces under their helmets, but I was little more than a cranky kitten to them, though my body and mind surged with the fury of ten tigers. *I've just killed a boy!*

"Fireflyyyyyy! Run!!" I screamed, writhing under their grip, but my horse disobeyed.

I saw a familiar, massive, hair-covered hoof out of the corner of my eye and instantly the guard to my left was dislodged from his hold on my arm and knocked out cold. The vapor snake, now gathering itself high above and searching for its next victim, coiled overhead and descended upon the guard who wrestled to still me. It slithered into his helmet, and vanished within his armor. The guard's grip weakened from my arm. I tore away, and he crumpled to the ground with a clatter. In moments, dark, sickly vapor issued with a hiss from the armor's cracks and was gone. The damage was done. The hex was spent. I kicked up his helmet and saw the death and terror etched into his unmoving face.

I staggered backward in horror. "We've got to get out of here. They'll come after us! We'll be executed!" I leapt onto Firefly's back, gathered Myriam's mare with a sharp command, and we charged to the southeast gate under the low, gathering storm clouds.

CHAPTER 25

Cold shadows stretched out across the hills; the sky darkened beneath a blanket of fat, gray rainclouds, which swallowed the smoky skeletons of the fairyworks.

My head reeled, replaying the horrible scene over and over as I raced to my wagon, to Aggie. She'd know what to do. When I crested the hill, I sucked in a sharp breath. The marketplace was empty, the entire village gone. The dark lake a horizontal mirror, pocked with tiny droplets of rain sending thin rings rippling outward.

All of the wagons should have already been outside the castle grounds on Steed Road heading to their next destinations, but they were lined up, and perfectly still. All of the people were gathered at the crest of the hill, facing me like soldiers about to attack. At the front stood Glyn, Fin and Myriam.

"Oh no. Oh, no, no, no." The reality of what lay behind me, stiff in the grass, took hold as I sensed the outrage in the faces before me. They saw. They saw everything! Firefly slowed and suddenly the only world I had ever known was sucked from me in a single breath.

Glyn's jaw muscled tight, he shook his head in the tiniest back and forth motion, disbelief and disgust coloring his eyes, mirroring the darkness of the gathering storm, and I wished... I wished it was me back there, dead on the ground. Seraphina sidled up next to him, took his hand in hers and squeezed it, leaning into him in a possessive way. And as if stuck in a slow-motion nightmare, I watched his fingers curl around her pale hand and squeeze it back. My mouth filled with that sour tang that comes prior to puking.

Aggie pushed her way through the crowd, holding a satchel and my bow and quiver, the furious look on her face shaming me. Penny abandoned us to join Myriam, while Firefly and I stood rooted to the meadow, time punishing us with its sudden slowness. A huge black cloud passed across the moons, casting a dark shadow across my people, a sea of silent, disapproving eyes boring into me. If they would have screamed or yelled, shook their fists at me, it would have been more bearable somehow.

Their silence, punctuated by peals of thunder, unnerved me completely. Aggie charged toward us, her feet barely touching the ground, illuminated now and again by jagged streaks of lightning like some tiny ferocious specter. I was frozen beneath her fixed gaze, and all I could do was wait and see what happened.

It has begun, whispered an Orphic voice on the gathering wind. The legend. I touched the itchy spot on my chest where the compass hid, holding my breath, waiting for a clue about what came next.

When Aggie was close enough that I could smell the familiar mix of herbs and potions that always lingered in her clothes and hair, her eyes were full of contempt, and she was foreign. She looked at me like I was a stranger, a criminal.

"The people have decided. The decision was unanimous and instant. Jesobel Vine, you are banished." She grabbed my arm and yanked me halfway off my horse, snatching my mother's circlet from my head, yanking out tangled hairs with it. I wanted to cry out, but I didn't dare.

"We will find another Starkeeper," she barked, releasing my arm and shoving a satchel onto my lap. "You're just lucky they've taken pity on you. Most of us wanted to hand you over to Rowan for your flagrant misuse of magic, your utter disregard for your own people's safety. How could you do this, Jesobel? How could you be so utterly careless? After everything I've taught you? What were you thinking?" For a fleeting millisecond, I saw a hint of the Aggie who raised me, but then she was gone, replaced by the furious Magic Weaver shoving my bow and arrow on top of the satchel. Firefly whinnied loud and long, stamping his foot as fat raindrops began to fall like wet comets.

The true gravity of what I had done finally began to sink in. It was bad enough, the worst thing ever that I killed two innocent people, but now I had also put my own people at serious risk. All of them. Across the entire globe.

My guts slipped around loosely inside of me, my nerves humming like a mouse's body before a cat pounces on it, my sense of reality fractured and broken. My quickflame. It crackled and popped in a painful way. It felt poisoned, dirty somehow. And I was the poison.

I wanted to say I was sorry, so, so sorry, but words weren't going to fix this. Nothing could fix this. I looked out at my people, and saw hatred burning in all of their eyes. When lightning cracked the sky apart, I secretly wished for it to strike me down.

Aggie set her jaw, cut her eyes at me—a stranger with a mob of strangers gathered behind her, ready to defend her. From what? From who? *From me*, I realized with horror. She stepped back, and raised her voice for all to hear, holding my circlet above her head, timing her words between peals of thunder and flashes of lightning, the rain gathering momentum.

"Jesobel Vine, you are banished from the Lost Realm of Pyxis for betraying your people and your duty as our future Starkeeper. You have shamed us. You have put us all in danger. You are dead to us, now. A ghost. Be gone!"

Glyn, my aching heart, was the first to turn his back on me, followed by a deeply saddened Fin and Myriam. And then, like some sort of single entity, my people turned their backs on me in unison, and I ceased to exist as they hurried to their wagons and moved them into a line out the gate to Steed Road.

Aggie gave me a hard, long look before she turned her back to me, her arm dropping heavily to her side, as if my circlet suddenly weighed as much as a mountain.

"Aggie, wait!" I screeched, not knowing what I was supposed to do. Heavy raindrops plummeted from the sky, pounding noisily on the grass—any second it would become an absolute deluge.

"Please!" I pleaded, urging Firefly to her side. "What am I supposed to do!"

I half hoped she would strike me down with some dramatic hex, but I knew death would be too kind a punishment, and she wouldn't offer me such an easy way out. Raindrops pelted her tight curls, making sinkholes in the silver halo like pebbles in candy floss, and for some reason, this tore at my heart so deeply that the rain became my tears, and I wailed, unable to control myself. "Aggie, please. Please look at me!"

She refused, and marched toward our wagon. *Her wagon.* Was I truly nothing to her now? I pushed Firefly to her side and reached for her small shoulder, spinning her to face me, but she refused to see me. I tried to position myself in her line of sight, but she looked through me.

Her eyes bored into the place on my chest where the compass hid. An eternity later, her voice met my ears through my sobs, as her hand reluctantly grasped mine, a small hint of warmth, which was wildly comforting. In a gravelly whisper-yell, she instructed me a final time.

"Go north toward the Percherons. Go, Jesobel. It's coming for you. It won't stop until it finds you. You have to find a way to prevail. I'm sorry you chose to do this alone."

"What is coming for me? What will happen when it finds me!" Terror skittered around my quickflame, I was wild with it, but Aggie flung my hand away and kept walking, and I was invisible again.

And then her sad, disappointed voice swept past in a gust of wind, taking my heart with it. "Use the compass. It will guide you." How was I supposed to use a compass that didn't even work properly?

With a deep breath, I urged Firefly toward the gate, and we shot past my people. We were a deliberately unseen streak of shame to a sea of baleful faces. I clenched my teeth, held my tears inside.

We thundered past my beautiful wagon sitting lonely and vacant, unhitched to any horse, gleaming with its freshly gilded scrollwork alone in the forest of signposts, waiting in vain to carry me off to my new life. I swallowed down a wave of nausea and bore toward the gate at a full gallop, abandoning my beautiful new home and everything I was meant to be. *Well, I guess you got what you wanted,* I scolded myself. *Almost.*

A childish and sickening thought consumed me as the southeast gate came into view through the column of dark posts and empty lanes we weaved between. A thought, that for no reason at all, hurt worse than every other horrible thought tumbling through me.

He's going to marry Seraphina.

Acknowledgements

There is an army of angels I'd like to thank for supporting me throughout this incredibly daunting process. Writing a book while battling PTSD is no easy feat. I couldn't have done it alone.

First, thank you to my beautiful boys, Forest and Cyrus, for believing in me and my imaginary planet no matter what. Special thanks to Jay and Guerin, whose spirits are always with me when I write. Huge amounts of gratitude goes to Juni who gifted me with a laptop to type the first three million drafts on, and who has cheered me from afar for an embarrassing number of years. Gigantic thanks to David, who believed in me enough to hire an amazing writing coach for me—I am forever grateful to you for this generous kindness.

Dax, you were the first person to read a bit of my book and excitedly tell me that I'd finally found my calling—I've repeated that moment over and over in my darkest hours. Thank you for believing in me so hard that I began to believe in myself. Thank you Linda, for loving me and encouraging me. And a huge thank you to Marlene—you will always be my Queen Starkeeper of Vale. Massive thanks to Goobie for sparkles, lovely words, and never letting me give up on myself. Special big thanks to my sister, Sarah, the Typo Killer, for proofreading this thing at atomic speeds, and Courtney Nuckels, who swooped in and saved the day with her awesome formatting skills and helpful spirit.

Enormous thanks to my tight circle of writing sisters—especially Jordan, who has been an incredible mentor, and Stephanie, whose humor has coaxed me off many a ledge. Frankie, who writes like a beast and inspires me to push harder, and who will always drool over Ian Somerhalder with me at two o'clock in the morning without complaint. Christina, my dearest fantasy-nerd sister and UtopYA Con booth-buddy whose constant moral support has meant more than she'll ever know. (Free covers for life, Christina!) Thank you to Erick, whose million trillion pep talks and never-wavering belief in me helped me press on time and time again. Thank you to Colleen, who has helped me believe in myself and who supports me with such love and understanding throughout my ongoing healing process. Gorgeous Collin, whose wisdom-packed pep talk by the pool made a deep and lasting impact on my journey towards self-love. Without learning this, I wouldn't have been able to finish this book!

Thank you to Luke, who has cheered me with cheesy lines from Steven Seagall movies countless times, and whose friendship I treasure. Janet Wallace, I can't even begin to thank you enough—you are my hero, my mentor, my tough love giver. Your guidance has fueled my drive to get shit done. I'm gonna make you proud! Thanks to Trudy Hale for the sanctuary that is The Porches, where so much of my story was conjured during quick little writing retreats. Laura and Minnette—my workout buddies and beautiful friends—I'm so blessed by your presence in my wacky universe! Susanna and Jen—I don't know how I could stand Charlottesville without you—you two are so fucking awesome! My wonderful neighbor Cindy and her family for cheering me on and helping out with Cyrus more times than I can count. My cover artist, Yu Cheng Hong, thank you for making me squeal with happiness when I saw my cover—I'm so excited to be working with you! And last but not least, thank you so very much to Nate for a multitude of things—especially for granting me time to write. And rewrite. And write and write some more.

ABOUT THE AUTHOR

Warrior, mermaid, wordsmith, performer for kings and queens, Chelsea Starling is fucking awesome. She raises bear cubs with one hand, and conjures whole worlds with the other.

Find out more at www.chelseastarling.com

Get Nyxiegrams in your inbox! Subscribe to the Nyxie Express! If you like the idea of being the first to know when the next book is released, or having access to exclusive scenes and other fun goodies, subscribe to the Nyxie Express! It's easy, I'll never spam you, and you can win cool stuff if your initials appear on the wax seal!

http://chelseastarling.com/the-nyxie-express/

www.ingramcontent.com/pod-product-compliance
Lightning Source LLC
Chambersburg PA
CBHW032139170626
46808CB00006B/2305